Huma

'He's just an animal, isn't he? Anyone with any ~~~~
But he walks upright and he looks a bit human, that's all. So I call
him humanzee, half-man, half-chimpanzee, see.'

'You can't put people in cages,' said Nemo, appalled. So he
persuades his parents to buy Chingwe, the humanzee, and
take him with them as they tour the country with their
travelling Flea Circus. But it is not so easy to cope with an
old and emotionally upset humanzee, especially when the
scientists want to experiment on him, and other people
object to his very existence and come after him with guns.
Nemo has to think fast to save Chingwe from the dangers
that are threatening him.

SUSAN GATES was born in Grimsby in 1950. She has a degree in
English and American Literature and a Dip.Ed from Coventry College
of Education. She is a teacher at a comprehensive school in County
Durham, and is married with three children.

Humanzee

Other books by Susan Gates

The Burnhope Wheel
The Lock
Dragline
Deadline for Danny's Beach
African Dreams
Raider
Firebug
Iron Heads

Humanzee

Susan Gates

Oxford University Press

Oxford New York Toronto

Oxford University Press, Great Clarendon Street, Oxford OX2 6DP

Oxford New York
Athens Auckland Bangkok Bogotá Buenos Aires
Calcutta Cape Town Chennai Dar es Salaam
Delhi Florence Hong Kong Istanbul Karachi
Kuala Lumpur Madrid Melbourne Mexico City
Mumbai Nairobi Paris São Paulo Singapore
Taipei Tokyo Toronto Warsaw

and associated companies in
Berlin Ibadan

Oxford is a trade mark of Oxford University Press

British Library Cataloguing in Publication Data
Data available

Cover illustration by Stuart Williams

ISBN 0 19 271796 0

Printed and bound in Great Britain by
Biddles Ltd, Guildford and King's Lynn

One

The fleas had finished feeding. I lifted them off my arm one by one, using a pair of tweezers. It was delicate work. You had to be careful not to squash them.

'Nemo, are those fleas ready?' Ma hissed at me through a flap in the tent.

'They're ready.'

Still using the tweezers, I picked the last flea up by the tiny wire harness round its body. I put it into the cigar box with the other fleas and closed the lid. It wasn't an ordinary cigar box. It was specially adapted, with rows of smaller boxes inside, one for each flea.

I rubbed my arm. It was a bit red where the fleas had bitten it. But it didn't hurt. You had to feed the fleas before a show or they got too frisky. Then they were hard to handle.

I was a good flea handler. I knew all the tricks. Another thing you could do—you know, to slow fleas down, stop them hopping all over the place—was to put them into an empty gin bottle. Just for a few minutes, until the fumes made them whoozy. Then you tipped them out again. They were easy to handle after that.

Anyhow, that particular day, the show seemed to be going as normal.

'What's the audience like?' I hissed back at Ma.

She poked her head through the flap and nearly knocked her hat off. It was a big black bonnet today, trimmed with curly ostrich feathers.

'What did you say, Nemo?'

'What's the audience like?'

'Ten people!'

1

That was a lot for us. You never got big audiences at those little country fairs. And ten was the most we could take, anyway. We're only a small operation. If you let more than ten people into our tent, it's a really tight squeeze—they start complaining they can't get a good view.

So, Ma's head disappeared again. The show was beginning! Pa had started his routine, warming the audience up, like he always does. He was telling them about the fleas—the ones in the cigar box that I'd just fed with my own blood.

'Ladies and gentlemen,' he was saying, 'I present to you the amazing spectacle of a circus in miniature. We have trained juggling fleas, tightrope walking fleas and even, ladies and gentlemen, chariot racing fleas. Their tiny chariots are pure gold. Made from the cogs and wheels of a fine lady's pocket watch . . . '

I knew Pa's spiel by heart—I'd heard it a hundred times before. That bit about us training the fleas wasn't exactly true. We didn't *train* 'em. You can't train fleas, it stands to reason—they've got no brains. But people always believed what Pa told them.

I stopped listening to Pa and looked round the fair instead. There wasn't much to look at—a bunch of tents and stalls in a dry, dusty field. Some pens with sheep and goats and long-horned cattle in them. A farmer walked past leading his prize bull.

It threw its head back, gave a great choking bellow: '*Maaaaaa!*'

'What's the matter, old lad?' the farmer asked it. 'You thirsty, are you?'

I thought, That's a stupid question. Of course it was thirsty.

The whole world is thirsty these days. No one can get enough water. Water's more precious than gold, than diamonds.

That reminded me that I was thirsty too. My throat seemed to be full of gravel. I swallowed a couple of times, then listened in again to see where Pa had got to. I didn't want to miss my cue.

'And, before we commence, ladies and gentlemen, I've got one last thing to tell you . . . '

There was a special kind of pride in Pa's voice. He'd got to the bit about Queen Victoria. He was inside the tent, I couldn't see him. I was waiting outside with my fleas. But I imagined Pa, waving his arms around, in his showman's clothes—his tartan waistcoat, moleskin trousers, and that red scarf knotted round his neck. He'd be twirling his moustaches now. The ends were waxed into little spiky tips. He always twirled his moustaches when he told this story.

'One day,' he was telling his audience, 'we were at a fair just like this one. Quite unknown to us, our dear queen was nearby with a royal shooting party. She spied our striped tent. She enquired of a local man, "My man, what is that tent?" "That, your majesty," replied the honest fellow, "is the Whirligig Flea Circus, famous at all country fairs and shows!" Our dear queen herself walked over. She graced our humble flea circus with her presence. She allowed our fleas to perform for her. And this, ladies and gentlemen, is what arrived afterwards, sent to us direct from Buckingham Palace!'

Ma would be bustling forward now. She'd be showing the audience the golden medal that said on it, 'By Royal Appointment, 1875'.

'Yes, ladies and gentlemen,' said Pa, 'we are the *only* flea circus in the world by royal appointment. And this medal is, of course, pure gold.'

'And if you believe that, you'll believe anything,' I murmured to myself, grinning.

But I was paying attention now, listening for my cue. I felt

3

that tingling inside, the same feeling I always get when it's almost time for my big entrance.

'You do not actually *need* magnifying glasses, ladies and gentlemen,' said Ma. 'The flea circus can be seen with the naked eye. But glasses are available, should anyone require them.'

'Now, gather round *perleese*, ladies and gentlemen,' said Pa inside the tent. 'Here is what you've been waiting for. Here is my son, Nemo, with the stars of our show. The tiny acrobats themselves!'

I took a deep breath, whacked a smile on my face and ducked inside the tent.

I liked putting on a slick show. I liked everything about it, especially the applause at the end. I could make it look simple. But it ain't simple, handling frisky fleas—not everyone can do it. This is how it worked: we got the fleas through the post from some bloke in Blackpool. He bred them specially. And when we got 'em they were already fitted with little wires; little harnesses fixed round their body so they were easy to handle. And I had to attach them, by these wires, on to our machines, our tiny bikes and chariots and things. That was the really tricky bit—you had to have cool nerves, steady hands. Take the cycling flea, for example. I wired him upside down on to the handlebars of the bike. And whenever you turn fleas upside down their legs go like mad. Now, on the bike, there was a little drum where the bicycle seat should be. And when the flea moved his legs the drum moved and the cycle wheels went round. And it looked like he was riding it, see? But he wasn't *really* riding it. It's just that, when he was all wired up like that, he couldn't help doing what he did.

It sounds cruel but it wasn't. It didn't hurt them, not if you were careful like I was. I loved my fleas. I looked after them. Fleas don't live long, only a few weeks. But mine had better lives than most human fleas. Regular meals and exercise and a nice warm cigar box to live in. Plus they were stars! But I don't think they cared about that, not like I do. I'm a natural showman, me. Just like my ma and pa. It's in our blood.

But I'm supposed to be telling what happened that day, when we got the news about Chingwe.

'Give Nemo room, please, ladies and gentlemen,' Pa asked the audience.

The farmers were pressed all around me. I could feel their hot breath on my neck. They smelled of straw and cow muck and sour milk. They shuffled back a bit.

In front of me, on a table, was the circus ring. Pa made it and painted it white. It looked like the real thing, only miniature. It was only about the size of a cart wheel. It had a little pole on a stand set up in it, ready for the first act—the juggling flea.

Using my tweezers, I took the juggling flea, very gently, out of the cigar box. A dozen pairs of eyes were fixed on me but my hands didn't shake. I fixed him by his harness upside down to the pole. Straight away his legs started going like mad. I took this tiny ball, light as a feather, that I made from the spongy pulp inside a willow branch. I dropped it on the flea's feet and, hey presto, it looked as if he was juggling it!

'Ally-oop!' said Ma as the ball spun faster and faster.

Pa took a penny whistle out of his pocket, started playing a jig.

'Well, look at that now,' said a farmer. 'Would you believe it? Look at that clever little beggar!'

The ball went slower. The flea was getting tired. I unfixed him and whisked him back into the cigar box. You have to keep your eye on them every second. They're really springy. If one escapes and someone in the audience starts scratching, that's very bad news.

'And now,' said Ma, her ostrich feathers bobbing, 'all of

5

you know of the craze for bicycling that is sweeping the country. Why, even some ladies are mounting these new machines! Cycling is becoming quite respectable! I can scarcely believe it but I hear our Prime Minister, Mr Gladstone himself, has taken a spin on a cycle.'

That was my cue to take the cycling flea out of his compartment in the box. He was already fixed to his tricycle. I lowered him, very delicately, into the ring.

'He's off,' said Pa, giving his waxed moustaches a twirl. 'Look at that tiny athlete fly!'

I was watching him like a hawk. Our circus ring had a gap in it, like real circus rings do. I didn't want him to cycle out of it and off the table.

'Burrp, burrp!'

The noise broke my concentration. Shit! I thought.

Then I realized what it was. It was Pa's mobile phone. He never usually left it on during a show. But that day was different.

'Burrp, burrp.'

I forgot about the cycling flea. Straight away I felt hot and queasy. Then icy cold, like I was in a deep freeze. My cycling flea rode out of the ring and off the table like he was cycling off the edge of the world . . .

I didn't even save him. He probably got crunched under some farmer's muck-loaded wellington boot. I was too busy watching every movement of my pa's face. When he'd finished the call his face looked sick and grey.

He ripped off his false moustache.

'Sorry, ladies and gentlemen, sorry,' he said to the people. 'Something's just come up. An emergency, family problems, life or death. We've got to cancel the show.'

Ma started taking off her costume. She pulled off her bonnet. Her hair was short and spiky and bleached snowy-white. She climbed out of her long Victorian skirt. She had tatty jeans and trainers on underneath.

The people were muttering. Some pushed their way out. Some didn't move. One said, 'What about our money back?'

Pa was trying to calm them down. But I didn't care about them any more. They weren't important. They didn't exist.

'Were they phoning about Chingwe?' I begged Pa. 'What did they say?' I was dead cool during the show when I was handling the fleas. I was in control. But now I could feel myself getting frantic. My hands started to shake—I just couldn't stop them.

'Yes,' said Pa, trying to keep his voice steady. 'It was about Chingwe.'

'We should never have left him there! I told you! I told you!'

'Shut up, Nemo,' said Pa. 'Just let's get going. Chingwe's being attacked. Dr Dekler said the others are trying to kill him.'

Two

'Get a move on!' I told Pa.

I wanted the van to go faster, faster. I was practically bursting with anxiety, jumpier than a thousand performing fleas. It was a life or death situation. We should be scorching along, burning up the motorway, overtaking Porsches.

But our old van was a joke. If you pushed the speed above sixty the steering wheel started to shake. It had WHIRLIGIG THEATRE COMPANY painted on the side in big rainbow letters. It looked like a kiddies' play-bus. No one who saw us trundling along could guess we were on an urgent rescue mission.

'We shouldn't have left Chingwe there!' I yelled at Pa for the hundredth time.

I was twisting my hoop ear-ring round and round in my ear. It hurt like hell but I didn't stop doing it.

Ma turned angrily round in her seat. She pointed her finger at me. 'Well, you tell me, Nemo, what choice did we have!'

''Course we had a choice!'

'Don't talk rubbish!'

'Just keep it quiet, you two,' said Pa, hunched over the wheel. 'You'll burst my ear-drums.'

Pa's the easy-going one. He's the one that keeps the peace. Me and Ma are too much alike, always flaring up, always striking sparks off each other.

Pa says, 'You could make anything into a drama you two, even passing the cornflakes.'

Suppose it's no big surprise really, because drama's our business.

We are the Whirligig Theatre Company.

Ma and Pa are community artists—that's their job. They do shows everywhere. In little country places that time forgot, in big city schools, in small-town community centres. And when I'm not at school, I help out. We do a lot of Victorian stuff—music hall, the flea circus, a play about kids working in factories. That's how I took to calling them Ma and Pa, like in Victorian times. But that's only part of our act. We do plays warning school kids about drugs, plays about bullying, one about the Blitz for old people's homes. We've got a show for every occasion.

We travel all the time. We're like nomads—never stay anywhere long. I've been to more schools than most kids have skipped breakfast.

So, there we were, rattling along in our old van, me and Ma letting rip with our feelings, Pa keeping his under control. But I knew he was worried sick about Chingwe, just like we were.

I felt something trickling down my neck. When I rubbed it my fingers were bright red. I'd been twisting my ear-ring so much I'd ripped my ear open. That's how worried I was.

'How far now? How far now?' I yelled at Pa.

Pa didn't answer. He just crouched over the wheel, stomped the accelerator to the floor. Our old rust-bucket van shuddered as if it was shaking itself to bits.

Usually Pa drives like an old lady; you know, very sedate. Reliant Robins speed past him on the road. But that day we went to get Chingwe, he was driving like a wild man.

'If they've hurt one hair of Chingwe's head!' Ma burst out. 'I'll make them sorry they were born!'

'Yeah, right!' I said fiercely 'I'll kill 'em! With my bare hands, I'll kill 'em!'

'Nemo,' warned Pa, hardly raising his voice. 'Just shut up.'

9

I looked out of the back window, tried to calm myself down. It was a tough challenge because I'm not a naturally calm person.

I made myself look at the scenery. There was no green anywhere. The drought made the countryside look brown and parched, really dreary. There was nothing to see. Nothing to take my mind off Chingwe.

So, as we drove on down the motorway, I couldn't help thinking about him. How his name was the name of an African Chief. How I'd found him huddled in a stinking cage, being shown as a freak. How the bloke who owned him was a real weirdo. It gave me the creeps just thinking about it.

We'd been in a seaside town, doing our Victorian flea circus show. That town was truly the pits. A cheesy dump on a stretch of coast so wild and windy and forgotten it was like the end of the universe.

No one wanted to go there, except of course, us, the Whirligig Theatre Company.

'It's what we're all about,' Ma says. 'Taking our shows to places where they never see live theatre!' She's a crusader, my ma.

So, there I was, in this dump, killing time between shows, wandering along the seafront. I saw this dark arcade with twinkling lights deep inside. It was called Wonderland so I sort of wandered in. It was the pits too. It had some old fruit machines and one of those games where grabby arms snatch at prizes. You never win at those; they're always fixed. And anyway, you wouldn't have wanted to win any of those prizes—faded fluffy toys and a few melted sweets and a heap of dead flies.

I was already thinking about walking out again when I saw a curtain at the back. It might have been white—once.

10

But it looked as if it hadn't been near a washing machine for a hundred years. Above this curtain there was a sign, written in big capitals, coloured in with kids' crayon. 'AMAZING FREAKS OF NATURE,' it said. 'Come and See the Show!'

Well, I'm a sucker for shows so I went in.

It wasn't live theatre, that's for sure, because they were dead freaks, not live ones. And they'd been dead for a long, long time. There was a two-headed kitten and a puppy with eight legs like a great big spider. They were pickled in glass jars. White and soggy and floating in yellow liquid.

Gross! I thought. It made my stomach heave. It was disgusting. It made the back of my neck crawl. All the same, it was kind of fascinating too.

I leaned forwards to take a closer look.

'Seen the merman?' a throaty voice said, right in my ear.

My heart flipped right over. I spun round to see who was there.

The man behind me was as white as the freaks of nature. He looked like he'd crept out from a cellar somewhere. He had a white greasy face. His big belly slobbed over his jeans. A bunch of keys clinked on his belt. He had piggy eyes buried deep in his face. But he didn't look like a threat—he looked friendly enough. He was even smiling.

I relaxed—just a bit. 'What merman?'

'Over there,' he said, jabbing with his thumb.

I turned round to look. A monster stared back at me. Something half-fish, half-man, with a scaly fish tail but a human body. It had a shrivelled shrunken head. Its mouth hung open.

'Is it real?'

The man laughed. 'All the kids ask me that!'

I couldn't take my eyes off the freak. 'Come on, it's a fake, isn't it?'

11

Then I had another idea. It made me feel hot and sick all over again. 'Hey, wait a minute! That top bit—it's not a dead baby, is it?'

The man sounded shocked. ''Course it's not! I wouldn't show things like that! What do you take me for? Anyhow, I wouldn't be allowed to. It's only an animal. Just a baby monkey, that's all. Look close, you can see that it is! Half a monkey stuck on to half a fish. Clever, ain't it?'

I didn't want to look closer. 'Yuk, that's gross! You shouldn't show things like that!'

He shrugged. 'Why not? What you getting so worked up about? It's just my little museum. It's educational, isn't it?'

'Educational!'

'Well, they're Victorian freaks, aren't they? Over a hundred years old, these freaks are. They did things like that then. 'Course,' he said, with this greasy smile, 'we wouldn't do things like that now.'

Then I heard it—a shuffling sound from somewhere behind me.

The man was already turning round, 'Hey, mate, want a Polo mint?' he asked someone.

I still felt queasy but I was curious, so I couldn't help looking too. And that was my first sight of Chingwe.

At first my brain felt like a big scribble. It couldn't sort out what I was seeing.

There was a cage. And a big sign over the cage that said 'HUMANZEE' in the same crayon letters as the sign outside. And inside the cage, standing upright, just like a man, was something . . . I couldn't tell what it was. It was about four feet tall and hairy all over like a chimp. But it had a horribly human head, small boned and delicate, not like a chimp's head at all.

It was an ape-man, a human chimpanzee, stuffed like the other freaks, the merman and the spider puppy.

At least, I thought it was stuffed. Until it moved.

It poked a black, wrinkled chimp's finger out of the bars and stuck it through the hole in the Polo mint. Then it pulled the mint back inside. Its lips came forward like a chimp to smack it up. Then it squatted down and stared at me out of desperately sad human eyes.

'What the hell is it?' I asked the man. My voice sounded strange, a sort of shaky whisper. 'Is it a human being? What you playing at? You can't put people in cages . . .'

''Course it's not human!' said the arcade man. 'You stupid or something?' He wasn't smiling any more. He didn't like being asked all these questions—he was turning nasty. 'I told you, I wouldn't put people on show! What do you think I am, a ghoul or something!'

'I thought, I thought—'

'He's just an animal, isn't he? Anyone with any brains can see that. But he walks upright and he looks a bit human, that's all. So I call him humanzee, half-man, half-chimpanzee, see. Just a harmless little con, that's all—'

'A harmless little con!' I was yelling the man's words back in his face. I was so mad I was practically fizzing. 'That's cruel that is! That's really cruel, keeping it shut up like that!'

The man's piggy eyes glowered. His chin jutted out. He got angry too.

'You don't know nothing!' he yelled back, pointing his finger at me like a spike. 'He's better looked after than he was before. I got him from a travelling showman. Right? The same old bloke I bought this lot from.'

His arm swept round the pickled freaks. 'You ought to have seen how that bloke kept him. So don't you tell me I'm being cruel! I didn't want no bloody humanzee, did I? But I was soft-hearted. I felt sorry for him, didn't I? I needn't have bought him but I did, didn't I? He'd be dead now if it wasn't for me,' he said jabbing his finger at me. 'So don't talk to me about being cruel! Right?'

13

He was barging me with his big belly. He just wanted to get me out of there, quick as he could.

But over his shoulder I could still see the humanzee, slumped on the floor of his cage. He had a big barrel chest and powerful shoulders, like chimps do. But his mangy grey head was nearly bald and his long arms and legs were scrawny. He looked like a broken-down old boxer, after his last fight.

'It's still cruel!' I told the man as he pushed me back through the curtain. 'It's still cruel!'

I felt so angry, so sorry for the creature that I could hardly speak. My throat was burning—it felt like it was on fire.

'I'll be back!' I promised the humanzee just before the curtain fell.

But the humanzee didn't even raise his head. He just gnawed on his knuckles, hopelessly.

I ran out of Wonderland. I ran, fast as I could, with my chest nearly bursting, along the beach, to where Ma and Pa were getting the flea circus ready for the next show.

Pa was sitting in front of the big make-up mirror gluing on his false moustache.

'Put that flap down, Nemo,' he said, as soon as I dived into the tent. 'Can't see what I'm doing.'

Some rays of light had slipped into the tent with me, making Pa's mirror into a sparkling sunburst.

Ma was tying on her Victorian bonnet. 'Those fleas haven't been fed yet. They'll be hopping all over the place. The show'll be ruined!'

'Where've you been?' said Pa.

I tried to tell him. But I was doubled-up, coughing. All I could do was tug at the back of his waistcoat. Then I got the words out. 'You got to come with me. You got to come! It's really urgent. I mean, really! There's something you got to see!'

'What's the matter,' said Pa, mildly. 'It can't be that urgent. We'll come after the show.'

I went crazy then, like a toddler having a tantrum. 'Now, now, now!' I shrieked at Pa, trying to push him out of the tent. 'I'm good, aren't I? I never ask you for anything, do I?'

Pa looked confused. 'What's that got to do with anything?'

But I was desperate, really frantic, petrified that I wouldn't be able to make my parents do what I wanted. That they'd gang up on me, close ranks, somehow stop me from saving the humanzee from that terrible freak show.

'Come on, come on, come on!' I gabbled at them, like a lunatic.

Pa stared at me, bewildered. But Ma said, 'Let's go with him. The kid's really upset about something.' I nearly threw my arms round her and kissed her.

Ma's face when she first saw the humanzee was just how I knew it would be—angry, disgusted, full of pity all at the same time. She said afterwards, 'I could've killed that arcade man!' She was class my ma. Like a fierce, wild woman! It was a great performance. She threatened him with all sorts—the police, the RSPCA, even with knocking his block off. And all this in a Victorian bonnet—the fake violets on it shivered every time she yelled.

The arcade man sold Chingwe to us for next to nothing, just to get Ma off his back. 'You're crazy, missus,' he warned her, as he took the money. 'I should be paying *you*! I'm glad to get rid of him. You don't know what you're taking on.'

Pa said, 'We know about animals. He'll be all right with us.' He sounded his usual calm self. But he wasn't. He was angry too. I saw a nerve twitching in his cheek.

I was so proud of my ma and pa. I've never been so proud of them as I was at that moment.

But the arcade man was 100 per cent right. We didn't have a clue what we were taking on. It *was* a crazy thing to

15

do, buying Chingwe. Because, after we bought him, that's when our problems really started . . .

I was thinking about all this as we were bouncing along in the van, running it through my mind, remembering how we'd found him and how, since then, he'd turned our lives upside down.

I was thinking, That was the first time Ma and Pa ever missed a show, when we bought Chingwe. And the second time is today. When we're going to rescue him.

Then Pa took a corner on two wheels. *Wham*, I clunked my head off the side of the van.

'Hey, Pa, watch out.'

'Don't kill us before we get there!' yelled Ma. 'We won't be much good to Chingwe dead!'

'We're here,' said Pa.

We were bumping along a dirt track. We passed a sign that said, 'Primate Rehabilitation Centre'.

Ma stopped gnawing her knuckles. Tried to leap out of the van before it stopped. She still had her Victorian ear-rings on, dangly and jet-black. The ones she'd worn for the flea show.

The fleas! I thought suddenly. Where'd I put them? I was so worried about Chingwe that I'd forgotten all about them. And they were my responsibility.

Then I remembered that I'd left them behind at the country fair.

A picture flashed through my mind, of them peddling their bikes, dragging their tiny chariots in the dark cigar box. Poor little circus stars . . .

Then I forgot them again. Because someone was running towards us. It was Dr Dekler, the Primate Rehabilitator. The scientist who told us he could socialize Chingwe with other chimps.

16

'Thank God you're here,' Dr Dekler said. He looked really flustered. 'Things have gone badly wrong. I've never seen anything like it. The other apes won't accept him. They've made themselves into a pack. They're hunting Chingwe down. They're trying to tear him to pieces!'

Three

We could hear the chimps before we reached the enclosure. They were making an incredible racket—whooping, barking, horrible high-pitched screams. There was a riot going on in there!

Dr Dekler hurried beside us. 'Of course, chimps hunt in the wild,' he was telling us. 'They eat meat; they hunt other apes and monkeys. But I've never seen that kind of behaviour here. And I've been studying them for twenty years.'

I was hardly listening. I was worried sick about Chingwe. We were at the enclosure now—it was full of dead trees and a couple of live ones, protected by electric wires. It had an electric fence round it so the chimps couldn't escape.

'*Boom, boom, boom!*'

I looked to where the noise was coming from. There were a dozen chimps in a big, shrieking gang. One was kicking an empty oil drum, '*Boom, boom, boom!*' and screaming and leaping high in the air. He was going crazy! His lips were stretched right back so his face was all teeth and gums. His canines were like Dracula teeth, deadly and razor sharp.

'That's Boss,' said Dr Dekler. 'He's the group leader. Chingwe has really upset him.'

'Where's Chingwe?' My eyes were flickering round, looking for Chingwe among the trees. I couldn't see him anywhere.

'An adult male chimpanzee,' Dr Dekler informed us, 'can crunch bones as efficiently as a panther.'

'Where's Chingwe?' I begged him.

Dr Dekler had taken a miniature tape recorder out of his pocket. 'Actually,' he said, 'this is quite fascinating.'

'There he is!' said Ma, pointing.

Chingwe was crouched against a dead tree, shrieking. The other chimps had him cornered. He was trembling with terror. He was holding out a shaking arm to Boss, palm upwards.

'Chingwe is making a submissive gesture towards Boss. He is begging for his life,' Dr Dekler told his tape recorder. His voice didn't have any expression in it at all.

But I was going frantic. 'Get him out of there! Get him out!'

'But Boss,' Dr Dekler recorded, 'has rejected the gesture. He is getting ready to charge.'

Boss wasn't very tall—about as tall as a ten-year-old kid. But when he dropped down on his knuckles, he looked really scary, more like a gorilla than a chimp. He had massive, powerful shoulders like a Sumo wrestler. His arms were set wide apart like a bulldog's front legs. He glared at the world out of tiny, hot, piggy eyes.

Those eyes reminded me of someone I knew. The arcade man—he had eyes like that.

Boss gave these two screechy, high pitched barks. *'Whop! Whop!'* He whopped his drum a couple more times. Then, *pow*, he exploded into action.

Behind him the chimps went berserk! Screaming and leaping and twisting in mid-air like big frogs. Boss raised dust like a charging rhino.

Chingwe tried to run. But he was weak. I mean, he'd been locked up in a cage for years. His joints were stiff, like an old grandad's. If he'd been human he would've had a Zimmer frame by now.

He couldn't escape—so he just covered his head with his hands. Boss sprang on to Chingwe's back. I couldn't believe it.

'Do something!' I yelled at Dr Dekler.

Boss was slapping and biting and kicking Chingwe in a mad fury. Then he sprang off and backed away. Chingwe was on the ground, writhing about.

'Boss has exerted his authority,' Dr Dekler droned into his tape, 'in a typical hit-and-run attack.'

Chingwe's shrieks seemed to slice through my brain.

'Chingwe is screaming for help,' recorded Dr Dekler. 'Note—he has an unusually high-pitched voice for a chimp. His vocalization is almost human.'

'Get him out! Get him out!' I was going demented. I couldn't bear it—just standing and watching! Chingwe's pitiful cries were breaking my heart.

'Do something!' yelled Ma, as frantic as me.

Pa said, in his calmer voice, 'You have to do something. We can't just *leave* him in there.'

Dr Dekler switched off his tape.

'No one can go in there,' he told us. 'It's a highly volatile situation. Boss will see it as a challenge. He'll kill whoever goes in there.'

'Chingwe!' I shouted. I was rushing to climb the fence when Pa pulled me back.

'It's electrified, son. Keep back!'

'I don't care! Let me go!' I yelled, fighting with Pa, struggling to tear myself free.

Chingwe had heard me yelling. He knew my voice. He looked up.

But Boss was picking up stones now, hurling them all over the place. He started slapping his chest and head.

Dr Dekler switched on his tape. 'Boss is preparing for another charge,' he recorded, in a solemn voice.

I just threw myself at him. 'Let me in there! Where's the way in? Switch off the electricity! I got to get in there!'

'No!' said Dr Dekler, trying to push me away. 'It's out of the question. I can't be responsible. And I can't interfere in ape society. That wouldn't be scientific.'

'You idiot!' Ma yelled, waving her arms around. 'We can't just stand here and watch him get killed!'

Pa kept his cool—how does he do that? I'll never know how.

'Look,' he said, in his reasonable voice, 'isn't there anything we can do? Can't we stop that big chimp without going inside? Divert him somehow?'

Dr Dekler thought about this—while Ma and me were going crazy, hopping about, we just couldn't keep still.

At last Dr Dekler said, 'They don't like water, or strong light dazzling their eyes—'

That was it. I was off, running for our van before he could even finish. I leapt into the back, chucked hats and costumes and props and stuff all over the place.

'Got it!'

I went racing back with the big make-up mirror under my arm.

'Good lad, good lad!' Pa chanted at me. 'Give it here!'

'I'll do it,' said Dr Dekler. 'Give it to me.'

He switched off his tape recorder, slid it into his pocket.

Boss was stamping about. He looked puffed up, swollen.

'He's bristling his hair,' said Dr Dekler.

He seemed twice as big, twice as dangerous. The other chimps crowded behind him, getting really excited. They were hooting—this horrible creepy sound. *'Hoooo, hoooo!'* It made your skin crawl.

Boss dropped down on his knuckles. And I knew exactly what he was doing. He was going in for the kill.

'Hurry up, dazzle him!' Ma yelled at Dr Dekler.

Dr Dekler took his time. He angled the mirror, very slowly, very carefully . . .

Boss skidded to a dead stop, rubbed at his eyes. Then he howled, threw himself on the ground, still howling.

'Run, Chingwe, run!' I shouted through the wire.

But if Chingwe understood me, he didn't run. He could

21

never have outrun Boss. He started walking, in that weird upright human walk, like a guardsman, with his hips and shoulders locked back.

'He's hurt. Look, Ma, he's hurt!' I yelled, pointing.

Chingwe started dragging one leg like a bird drags a broken wing. He was staggering about.

'I don't think so,' said Dr Dekler, still zapping Boss with the mirror.

'But he's limping,' Ma said. 'Any fool can see that!'

'Just watch,' Dr Dekler insisted.

The other chimps had stopped screaming. They made these soft whooping noises, 'Oo, oo, oo,' when they saw Chingwe limp by. But they didn't try to hurt him. They drew back and let him go. Soon as he was safely past them, Chingwe started to run.

'Amazing!' said Dr Dekler. 'Did you see that? He was play-acting, bluffing! Pretending to be injured so they'd think he was beaten. So they wouldn't attack!'

He was so excited he let the mirror slip and quicker than you could wink Boss was on the move again. He was big and bulky like a bear. But when he moved—he was fast as a leopard.

'Dazzle him!' snapped Ma.

But Boss was too quick.

Chingwe saw he was being chased. He ran for the wire. The other chimps went hysterical! They made an ear-splitting din—hooting, screaming, barking, bashing the oil drums. Chingwe looked round. His lips were stretched back in a ghastly grin. He was terrified out of his mind.

'Chingwe!' I yelled, desperately.

'I'll turn the fence off,' said Dr Dekler, suddenly.

His open-topped jeep was parked near the fence. He jumped into it, went roaring off. I didn't see where, I was too busy watching Chingwe.

Chingwe was still running. He was running on his

heels—this weird rocking run, with his long arms dangling down. He didn't stand a chance against Boss.

'Boss is going to catch him!'

With my Dad's 'No, Nemo!' ringing in my ears, I threw myself at the wire fence. I didn't strike sparks. The electricity was off. I started climbing up it, yelling, 'Chingwe! Chingwe!' so he'd know I was coming to save him.

I hauled myself over the top, dropped down on the other side. I was rolling in the dust, the breath slammed out of my body.

I looked up. And saw Boss's massive square head, his brow jutting out like car bumpers. And his great yellow doggy teeth.

'Crouch back down!' someone was yelling from outside the wire. I swivelled my head round, very, very carefully. It was Dr Dekler, braking his jeep in a cloud of dust. 'Don't look in his eyes. He'll think it's a threat!'

I cowered down, my heart hammering, put my hands over my eyes. But I could still see, through my fingers.

Outside the fence Dr Dekler was tilting the mirror. Boss shrieked.

'Run, Nemo!' Pa shouted.

I was already scrambling to my feet ready to run when a leathery hand fitted into my own. I whipped my head round and it was Chingwe peering into my face.

'I'm all right,' I told him.

He just stood there.

'Come on. Look, Chingwe, like this.'

I started to climb the wire fence. 'Come on, Chingwe. Do like I do!'

After we bought him from the freak show, before we tried ape rehabilitation, Chingwe just didn't respond. We tried everything. Ma said, 'He's a seriously disturbed chimpanzee.' He rocked to and fro, to and fro, for hours on

23

end. Except sometimes he had temper tantrums, like toddlers do. He'd roll around and scream and beat the ground. But sometimes, only sometimes, he'd copy you, like a baby does. If you pointed at him, he'd point back. If you waved, fluttered your hand about, he'd wave too.

I wanted him to copy me now. 'Come on, Chingwe, you can do it.'

And he did. He started to climb the fence. 'Good boy, Chingwe.'

It flashed through my mind, If Chingwe can copy, maybe Boss can too. But I didn't want to think about that.

'The sun's going in!' yelled Dr Dekler. 'Hurry up, the mirror's not working!'

I swarmed over the top, down the other side, all the time coaxing Chingwe, 'Come on, boy, come on.'

He was no good at climbing. He climbed really clumsily, as if it hurt him. He was all long, spidery arms and legs, hooky fingers and toes.

Boss could get up that fence in ten seconds.

'They're down!' yelled Pa. 'Get the electricity back on!'

Dr Dekler was already zooming off in his jeep.

I could hear Boss roaring. I turned round to look. He was standing up, banging his chest like Tarzan.

Then he dropped to his knuckles and scooted towards the fence sideways like a giant crab. I thought, He's gonna climb it! I yelled to Ma and Pa and Chingwe, 'Get running!'

Boss was in a raving, red-hot frenzy. He was going to rip our heads off.

Boss hit the fence side on—wallop. And bounced off, screaming. Dr Dekler had thrown the switch and made the fence live again.

Boss was curled up on the ground, twitching, whimpering like a hurt child. The other chimps crowded round him, making worried hooting noises, 'Oo, oo, oo.' Some hugged him; some offered him leaves to eat.

But I didn't care about Boss. All I cared about was Chingwe.

And Chingwe was having a mega temper tantrum. He was going ape.

'Gerroff! Gerroff!' I yelled, ducking, as he stamped and screeched and pelted me with lumps of soil. 'It was a mistake, OK? We shouldn't have left you there! We thought you'd like it there with the other chimps, didn't we? We didn't know what would happen. How did we know? Hey, *ouch*, that hurt, Chingwe. Stop chucking those stones!'

Dr Dekler came hurrying back, just as Chingwe wore himself out. He just crumpled into a hairy heap, hugging himself, yelping, 'Yip, yip, yip, yip.' He was still making his fear-face. He was very stressed out. I didn't blame him. I'd only been in there a few minutes with Boss and I was a nervous wreck.

'It's all right,' I told him. 'You're safe. Boss can't get you now.'

You couldn't even see Boss and the other chimps. They'd taken cover amongst the dead trees.

'He's scared out of his wits, poor thing,' said Ma. 'We're not leaving him here in this hell-hole.'

'Right, Ma!' I said. 'No way! He's coming home with us!'

'Now wait a minute,' said Pa. 'Just wait a minute here. Let's use some common sense. We had Chingwe two weeks, before we brought him here. We tried. But we couldn't cope. We decided, didn't we—he needs expert care.'

'I'll give him that,' said Dr Dekler. 'Leave him with me—'

'No way! No way!' I interrupted him. I was really outraged. 'You'll put him back in there with Boss.'

'I won't put him in there.'

'No way!' The thought of leaving Chingwe here made me shake with rage and fear.

'Just listen, Nemo,' urged Pa. 'Stop getting yourself so worked up, just for one minute. We've got to think what's best for Chingwe. He's a seriously damaged chimp—you know, in his mind,' said Pa tapping his own head with one finger. 'And he's not physically strong either, is he? He's got all sorts of problems—'

'We're not leaving him here!'

'I won't put him in the enclosure again,' promised Dr Dekler. 'He's far too precious.'

'What do you mean "precious"?' asked Ma.

'Well,' said Dr Dekler, rubbing at his chin thoughtfully. He glanced at Chingwe but Chingwe had gone back to rocking again, backwards and forwards, backwards and forwards. 'I'm changing my mind about him. At first I thought he was some kind of mutant chimp—a mutant bonobo chimp, probably. That's why he looks different, why he walks upright. But there are other signs now—the way the other chimps reject him—he even smells different from them—his superior intelligence. I think he might be something special. Even a major, and I mean major, discovery.'

'I discovered him!' I protested. I didn't like Dr Dekler muscling in on my chimp. I didn't trust him. 'I already knew he was special!' I told Dr Dekler. 'And even before I discovered him that arcade man knew he was special. He put "HUMANZEE" on his cage. He said he was an ape-man, half chimp, half man. He already knew that!'

'Humanzee?' said Dr Dekler, his eyes brightening. 'That's very interesting because that's what I suspect he is too. Chimps are our closest living relatives. And somewhere along the line, maybe four or five million years ago, some of them started walking upright. They started to evolve into humans. Archaeologists are always digging for those missing links. You know, skeletons that show how apes turned into men. Well, I think they're looking in the wrong place. I think we have a missing link here, above the

26

ground. I think we have a *living* missing link! This chimp could be an evolutionary bombshell!'

For once, me and Ma didn't know what to say.

Finally Ma managed a few words. 'So Chingwe's really important, right?' she said, frowning.

She scrubbed at her white, hedgehog hair. Then she wrinkled her nose at Pa as if she was asking him, 'So . . . what do we do now?'

'He might be important,' said Dr Dekler. 'I'm only saying *might* be, of vital importance to evolutionary science. Of course, I could be wrong. I could be way off the mark—only extensive scientific experiments will tell.'

'You want to *experiment* on him?' I blurted out, really shocked.

I ran over to Chingwe, put my arms round his shaking shoulders.

'Is he crying?' asked Dr Dekler, his voice rising in excitement. 'Are those tears? That's quite amazing. Chimps can't cry. Only humans cry.' He took out his tape recorder.

Quickly, I dried Chingwe's grey muzzle with my sleeve. 'He's not crying!' I told Dr Dekler fiercely. 'He's just got watery eyes that's all. And anyway, what experiments do you want to do? He's not staying here to be experimented on!'

'There's no need to worry,' said Dr Dekler soothingly. 'No need at all. We wouldn't hurt him. We'd keep him in strict isolation, away from other chimps. We'd do genetic testing. For example, humans have forty-six chromosomes, chimps have forty-eight. What if Chingwe has forty-seven? I'm only speculating here—but you've no idea how exciting that would be. I could make this ape famous,' said Dr Dekler with a dreamy look in his eyes. 'Really famous. Also, we'd do some tests on brain function—'

'Hey, wait a minute!!' A terrible image had sprung into my mind, of a photo I'd seen somewhere, of monkeys in a

27

lab with probes sticking out of their brains. I went crazy then. I went totally berserk. 'You're not opening up his brain, you bastard!'

'Nemo,' warned Pa.

Dr Dekler looked shocked. 'We wouldn't do that. A few sensors perhaps, while he performs some intelligence tests—'

I didn't want to hear any more. I blocked up my ears while I yelled, 'No, no, no! He's coming with me. Nobody's doing experiments on him! He's my humanzee, not yours. Tell him, Ma, tell him!'

'Nemo,' said Pa, shaking his head helplessly. 'Have you thought about this? Dr Dekler knows about apes. He won't hurt Chingwe. It might be better to leave him here—'

I could feel them ganging up against me. I turned wildly to Ma. 'Tell him, Ma!' I said, desperately. 'Tell him! You're on my side, aren't you?'

'It's not a question of sides—' Pa started to say. But I wasn't listening to him. I was watching Ma's face.

For a second I thought she was going to let me down. She wasn't like other kids' mothers. And sometimes I wished she were. But today wasn't one of those times. I didn't think other kids' mothers would let them keep a living missing link.

Ma screwed up her face. That meant she was thinking hard. All my Ma's feelings showed on her face, like a little child's do. Then her face smoothed out, as if she'd made up her mind.

She told Pa, 'We can't do it. We can't leave him here. It's wrong, I just feel it's wrong. I mean, we only left him to see if he could live with other chimps. But he can't, can he? So he doesn't belong here.'

Pa sighed, 'What makes you think he belongs with us?'

I opened my mouth to protest but Pa waved his hand for me to be quiet. 'All right, all right,' he said. 'I don't think this is the right place for him either. But that doesn't mean we don't go on searching. We keep him, but *only* until we find somewhere better to take him—'

'Yes!' I interrupted, leaping up and punching the air. 'Yes!' I was wild with happiness. 'Right!' I said to Chingwe. 'We're outta here.'

'Wait,' said Dr Dekler. His voice didn't sound so friendly now. 'I just hope you know what you're doing. I ought to warn you, if you take Chingwe away, priceless scientific data will be lost. It may be too late to collect it.'

'What do you mean "too late",' demanded Ma, suspiciously.

'Chingwe's old,' said Dr Dekler. 'He's got rheumatism in his joints. He may well be over forty. In chimp terms that's a very old man.'

'I see,' Pa said, frowning.

'What's that got to do with anything?' I said, terrified that it would make Pa change his mind. 'I don't care if he's old. He's still coming with us. You want to experiment on him! You want to open up his brain!'

'Shut your mouth, Nemo,' said Ma. 'Just get Chingwe in the van.'

I shut up. I'd got what I wanted. And Ma can get vicious if you push her too far.

Pa said, sort of apologizing, 'Look, I'm sorry but I still think we ought to take him with us.'

'I can't stop you,' said Dr Dekler. 'But you're making a mistake. He may be a terrible loss to science.'

I took Chingwe's hand. I just wanted to get him away from there, as fast as possible. 'Come on, come on,' I told him, impatiently. But I couldn't hurry him up. He was still in a mood, dragging behind me like a sulky kid. Then I heard Dr Dekler say something else. I couldn't believe it. It stopped me dead in my tracks.

'Can I ask you one last thing?' said Dr Dekler. 'When the

29

ape dies, could you get in touch with me? I'd like to have his body—or at least his skeleton.'

I just couldn't believe my ears. Was he serious? I mean, how dare he? How creepy is that? What a ghoul. But his voice sounded completely normal, like he was asking for a chocolate bar in a shop.

Even Pa looked surprised. He was mumbling some kind of reply—I couldn't hear what.

But I wasn't going to mumble. I opened my mouth to *yell*. I'd got a whole collection of insults ready.

But just as the first word came bursting out, Ma grabbed me by the scruff of the neck—she's skinny but sometimes she's really strong—and yanked me towards the van.

'Come on, Nemo,' she said, sighing and raising her eyebrows. 'That's enough now. Give your mouth a rest. Time to get going.'

As we drove away, Dr Dekler stood and watched us. I felt like putting up two fingers at him. Poking out my tongue and yelling, 'Ya! You didn't get Chingwe!'

But that would have been *amazingly* childish. And besides, Ma was watching.

So I just stared at him out of the rear window of the van. And before he got hidden by a cloud of orange dust, he stared back at me. I didn't like the look he was giving me. I thought it was hard—and unforgiving.

Four

The Whirligig Theatre Company was driving through the night. We were taking Chingwe far away from the Primate Rehabilitation Centre, back to our base, in the North.

But first we went back to the country fair. We had to take down the flea circus tent, pick up the other stuff we'd left behind in our mad panic to rescue Chingwe.

I didn't want to open that cigar box. But I had to.

The chariot fleas were dead. The tightrope walking flea looked poorly. And where was the juggling flea? I couldn't find him anywhere.

I felt really sorry about it.

'They're only *fleas*,' I kept telling myself. 'Don't be so soft. They don't live long anyway.'

But they were fellow performers. And it was my responsibility to look after them. I couldn't help feeling sad, could I?

I still felt embarrassed though—as if other kids were watching me, laughing at me. I was sure other kids wouldn't have got so depressed over a few dead fleas.

I'd been thinking a lot about other kids lately. About what they thought of me. About how different I was from them. I wasn't *surprised* I was different. Ma and Pa had been telling me that all my life: 'We're the Whirligig Theatre Company. We don't care what other people think! We're different!'

They were proud to be different. And I was too, at first. I mean, I'm not shy; I'm the extrovert type. I'm a showman. Being different wasn't a problem.

Except, three weeks before, we'd been at a city youth club doing our play about Victorian workhouse children and how badly they were treated. There were some tough, scary kids in the audience. I could see that when they were coming in. But, soon as the play started, I forgot about them. I love that play. I always get really involved in it. I play Spike—this boy who's starved and beaten by the brutal workhouse superintendent (played by Pa) and who ends up dying in the snow of TB. It's tragic. So there I was, dressed in rags like Spike would have been, coughing my guts up, playing Spike's death scene. I was putting my heart and soul into it, nearly crying myself I was so moved. I was in a world of my own. Like I said, I'd forgotten about the tough kids in the audience. Then suddenly, I heard sneery giggling from the front row.

'Tee hee hee.'

That was it, my concentration went. I wasn't Spike any more. I couldn't help looking to see who'd laughed.

It was three girls about my age, about thirteen. They looked tough and cool and streetwise. They had mocking eyes.

I could hear what they were saying. I think they meant me to hear. They didn't even bother to whisper.

'What a show-off,' one said. 'He really fancies himself!'

'He's going bananas,' sniggered the other one. 'Look at him, getting really carried away.'

'What *does* he think he looks like? Talk about over the top!'

I should've shrugged it off. I should have forgotten it. I mean, how can I fancy myself when I'm playing Spike? I'm Spike then, not Nemo. I'm not even *thinking* about Nemo. So that bit was stupid for a start. But I couldn't forget what they'd said. Not any of it. I remembered every single word, as if they were burned with acid into my brain.

And I was remembering those words as I stuck the tightrope walking flea on my arm and let it suck my blood.

Those girls, I was thinking, they'd really take the piss out of you, getting worked up like this over a few fleas.

It didn't even matter whether the fleas lived or died. Because the flea shows were over for a while. The Whirligig Theatre Company—with Chingwe—was heading home for a break.

Ma was driving. I'd lost track of time. There was nothing to see out of the rear window, only headlights whizzing past in the dark. I was in the back of the van with Chingwe. Pa was snoring his head off in the passenger seat. When we got off the motorway, on the small twisty roads, Pa woke up.

'Where are we?' he asked Ma.

'Not far,' said Ma. I peered out of the rear window. I couldn't even see car headlights now. Not a single light twinkling in all that blackness.

'It'll be good to see the old place again,' Pa said.

We hadn't been back home for three weeks. We'd been on the road all that time, since the beginning of my school summer holidays.

'When we get home,' said Ma, 'the first thing I'm going to do—the very first thing before I crash into bed—is to drink some water from Hope Spring.'

'Magic,' said Pa, rubbing his hands. 'I can taste it now.'

Hope Spring had a taste all its own. Ma said it tasted of flowers.

The Whirligig Theatre Company was always broke, never had any spare cash. But we had one valuable thing—water. Our base was Broom Cottage, in the North, high up in the hills. No water company pipes reached there. But we didn't care about that. We didn't need the water companies. Because Broom Cottage had its own water supply. It had natural spring water, bubbling up from Hope Spring.

'Remember that city?' Pa said. 'There were stand-pipes in the streets. They were actually fighting over water—'

'These days,' Ma interrupted, 'water's worth more than gold, than diamonds. People will kill each other for water! Hope Spring is the most precious thing we've got—'

It was my turn to interrupt. 'What about Chingwe!' I protested angrily from the back of the van. 'Dr Dekler said he was precious. He said he's a missing link—well, he might be. He said scientists would kill to get their hands on him. But they're not gonna. No way! I'll kill them first —'

'Calm down, Nemo,' said Pa automatically. 'Nobody's going to hurt him.'

'We've got two precious things then,' yawned Ma—she'd been driving a long time. 'Hope Spring and a humanzee. We're rich.'

The swaying van and the darkness made me dozy. Half-asleep, I started to give my head a good scratch.

Chingwe shuffled closer. He peered at me. He seemed really interested.

Just five minutes ago, Chingwe hadn't looked like a humanzee at all. He'd looked 100 per cent chimp. He'd been squatting on the van floor eating a grapefruit. He loved grapefruit—the pink ones were his favourite. He'd turned it inside-out with grabby fingers, made his mouth into a funnel shape and sucked in the pink juice like a vacuum cleaner. Then he'd smacked his wide, rubbery lips.

I did a bit more scratching.

Chingwe shuffled a bit closer. He started lifting up my hair. I could feel his fingers gently sorting through it.

'Hey!' I said. 'What you doing?'

Chingwe had found something. Delicately, he trapped it between his finger and thumb. He held it out, as if he wanted me to admire it.

I squinted at it. Put my nose right up against it. Saw tiny waving legs and an almost invisible harness made out of wires, thin as cotton—

'No, Chingwe! That's one of ours! That's the juggling flea!'

Too late. Chingwe had already popped the little circus star, plus harness, into his mouth.

'Oh, Chingwe!' I sighed, shaking my head.

But, this time, I was too excited to be upset about the flea.

'Pa!' I yelled, as if he was miles away, not sitting close enough to touch. 'He groomed me. Chingwe groomed me, like I was another chimp!'

Pa pretended to rake out his ears, 'No need to shout.'

Ma laughed, 'Well, like Dr Dekler says, you are his closest living relative.'

But I was thrilled. I felt really privileged. 'He groomed me. That shows he likes me, Ma. He's glad to be back with us.'

The sky was streaky with grey and pink. Dawn was coming up. We'd driven right through the night. We were on our home patch now. The landscape all round us was rocky grey limestone. Once, before global warming really kicked in, the grey rocks had been silvery with streams. There'd been water gushing all over the place. But drought had dried most of them up. The whole world was in big trouble over water. There wasn't enough of it. Even here, in the North, water companies couldn't supply the demand.

That's why Hope Spring was more precious than diamonds. It didn't dry up. It came from deep underground, through cool limestone tunnels. And it was our private spring, on our land.

'We're nearly home, Chingwe,' I told him. 'After all that travelling.'

Chingwe was hooting gently to himself, 'Hoo, hoo, hoo,' and doing his usual rocking, with his head buried in his arms.

'Don't be scared,' I told him. 'You'll be all right now. And don't worry—we'll never send you back to that primate rehabilitation place.'

Chingwe fell asleep, just closed his eyes, *zonk*, like a tired baby does. He was cuddled up against me. I could feel my eyelids getting heavier—

'Right!' yelled Ma. She slammed on the brakes.

I woke up with a jerk. 'Hey, whatsamatter!'

'First things first,' said Ma.

She leapt out of the van. We were right in front of our house, Broom Cottage. But Ma didn't go in the front door. She disappeared round the back.

I couldn't help grinning. I knew what she was going to do. She always did the same thing when we came home after a long tour—it was like a ritual. She made her hands into a bowl shape and scooped them into the deep crystal pool where Hope Spring bubbled up out of the ground. Then she drank a few sips of water and splashed the rest over her face and head so the drops shone like jewels in her hair.

I felt hot and sweaty and thirsty after hours in the back of the van. I thought, I'm going to do that too.

I could already taste our spring water, cold and tangy in my mouth.

I jumped out and followed Ma.

When I walked round to the back of Broom Cottage, Ma wasn't kneeling by the pool, splashing water. She was standing staring down into it with her hand clenched over her mouth. I joined her and stared down too. Neither of us spoke. We were too shocked—we just couldn't believe it. There was no water sparkling in the pool. Nothing but dry pebbles and dust in the bottom of it.

Ma finally spoke. 'It can't be true,' she said in a dazed voice. 'Nemo, am I really seeing this? I thought Hope Spring would never dry up.'

Pa came round into the back yard. He was trailing Chingwe by the hand.

'Look, it's dried up,' Ma told him, even though he could see for himself.

We all stood round the edge of the big, empty pit. Chingwe copied us, looking down too, with the same horrified look on his face, as if he understood what was going on.

'It's a disaster,' said Ma. 'We can't live here any more. Not without water.'

I turned angrily to Pa. 'I thought you said Hope Spring would never dry up!'

'It hasn't dried up,' he said. 'Underground aquifers like this don't just dry up. This isn't because of the drought. Someone's done this to us. Someone's stolen our water supply.'

Five

Ma was raving, practically foaming at the mouth. 'They're a bunch of outlaws! A load of crooks! They'll stoop to anything. Even stealing other people's water!'

She was talking about the water company, Aqua North. Water was big business. 'Anything to line the pockets of their greedy shareholders!' Ma fumed.

She and Pa were convinced Aqua North had interfered with our water supply.

'They've sunk a bore hole somewhere,' said Pa. 'They're probably pumping it out, sending it down the pipeline to the nearest town.'

'I can't see anything,' I said, looking out of the window of Broom Cottage. All I could see was the Whirligig Theatre Company van and, past that, craggy grey rocks, twisted trees, and the bright yellow splashes of gorse bushes.

'Well, you won't, will you?' said Pa. 'I don't know where Hope Spring comes from. There's a maze of tunnels and caves under these hills. They could be pumping it up miles away and we'd never know.'

Pa made another phone call. He'd been phoning Aqua North since nine o'clock, making accusations, trying to get some action.

'Give me the phone,' said Ma. 'I'll shake them up!'

But even Ma got nowhere. 'It's like bashing your head on a brick wall. They say they don't know anything about it!'

'They would say that, wouldn't they?' said Pa. 'They—'

'And anyway, how would our little bit of water make any difference!' I interrupted him angrily. I felt really outraged. 'Who do they think they are? Stealing *our* water? What they

38

playing at, the stupid morons? They're total crooks, they are! They should be shot! *Rat, tat, tat, tat, tat!*'

I mimed raking a row of Aqua North officials with a machine gun.

But instead of agreeing with me, saying, 'Yep, that's what they deserve', Pa just got annoyed. 'Nemo, will you stop going over the top?' he said. He punched in another number. 'Just stop going ape, right? I'm trying to concentrate here.'

I made a gibbering monkey face at him. 'I'm not going ape. I'm just saying the truth, that's all. I'm saying how I *feel.* I hate that water company! I can't help my *feelings,* can I? Why are you saying I'm going ape when it's how I really feel?'

'It's just that getting carried away,' said Ma, wearily, 'isn't very helpful right now.'

Even Ma wasn't backing me up. She turned back to Pa and said in a worried voice, 'We'll have to get some emergency water supplies from somewhere. Until we can sort this thing out.'

'Come on, Chingwe,' I said in disgust. 'Let's get out of here.'

It's stupid but I felt really upset. I'd never thought I was over the top. It never even occurred to me. Not until those girls had said it. And now Pa and even Ma were saying it too. My mind was all shaken up, full of doubt and confusion. To tell the truth, before everyone started saying I was over the top, I thought I was quite cool. If I'd been doing one of those magazine questionnaires—where you have to tick words to describe yourself—I'd have ticked 'cool', no question.

And the other thing that really bothered me was this. All those years, I'd been part of the Whirligig Theatre Company, travelling round, putting my heart and soul into shows, giving it 200 per cent, thinking I was doing a great job. When all the time, other kids were laughing at me, saying,

'Look at him! He really fancies himself. He's really over the top.'

It was a truly painful discovery. It really hurt, like a punch in the guts.

'You fool!' I sneered at myself as I walked out of Broom Cottage with Chingwe. 'They were all laughing at you and you never realized. Every time you acted, like in Spike's death scene, they were killing themselves laughing. You were a big joke, ha, ha, ha. Why didn't you *realize*!'

I was furious with myself. I couldn't believe I'd been so dumb for so long. The embarrassment of it made me squirm. The thought of how blind and naive I'd been made me nearly physically sick. 'You're thirteen!' I told myself viciously. 'But you didn't have a clue, did you? You must be the most clueless thirteen-year-old kid in the whole wide world, in the universe.'

'Well, I'm learning fast,' I told Chingwe. 'I'm not going to be as dumb again, no way. I'm not being Spike again for a start. Ma and Pa can't make me. And if they try to, I'll just tell them where to go!'

I felt angry with Ma and Pa too, like they'd somehow betrayed me, set me up for all this heartache by making me proud to be different.

'Even my name's embarrassing,' I told Chingwe, bitterly.

I once asked Ma and Pa why they called me Nemo.

'You're named after Captain Nemo, from the book, *Twenty Thousand Leagues Under the Sea* by Jules Verne,' said Ma, as if it was the most natural choice in the world. 'We wanted your name to be different.'

'From now on,' I told Chingwe, as we hung around together outside Broom Cottage, 'I don't want to be different. I just want to be normal. If you see me being different or getting carried away, stop me, right? I don't want to go ape. If you see me going ape, stop me. Right?'

'Oo, oo, oo,' said Chingwe, scratching himself under

40

both armpits. He had a twig in his foot. And he was poking it into a heap of dirt. He pulled the twig out and sniffed at the end.

His wrinkled old face looked up at me. He didn't have car bumper eyebrows like Boss. Or bandy bulldog legs. When he walked it was upright like a man. He *looked* more human than other chimps, no question. He cried when other chimps didn't. But it was hard to tell what he really understood.

'Are you a humanzee?' I asked him. 'Are you the missing link, like Dr Dekler said?'

I didn't know. And Chingwe wasn't telling.

A blackbird zoomed overhead, chattering. 'Hoo, hoo, hoo!' Chingwe covered his head and gave his alarm call.

He was scared of everything. Years of captivity had made him a nervous wreck.

I squatted down next to him. 'It's OK. It's only a bird, it won't hurt you.' But he still moaned and rocked. It was pitiful, I couldn't stand to see him like that. I wanted him to be happy. I put an arm round his shaking shoulders, trying to make him stop.

'It's all right, it's all right.' I wiped his tears away with my sleeve, cradling him like he was a frightened baby, crooning to him. 'It's all right, it's all right, it's all right—'

Then a thought turned everything sour. I heard *their* voices inside my head, 'What *does* he think he looks like?' Those girls would say that, with their mocking eyes. Embarrassed, as if they were watching, I stopped trying to comfort Chingwe. I jumped up and moved right away from him.

I walked to the edge of the pit and looked in. I should have been looking at a deep pool of clear, bubbling water. But the pit was dry as a bone. I booted a couple of pebbles in. One of them didn't clink on the bottom. Instead it bounced, then shot through a gap in the rock.

Hey, I thought, that must be where Hope Spring comes up, through that hole.

41

I'd never noticed it before—it was usually deep under water.

Then another idea snapped into my brain. I told Chingwe, 'There are tunnels and caves down there. Pa said so. If I could get down there, if I could follow those tunnels, maybe I could find out where the water company is stealing our spring. What do you reckon?'

Chingwe sucked on a grass stalk. He didn't have many teeth left. He scratched his mangy, nearly bald, head with his foot. If he was a missing link, he was a pretty decrepit one. He pretended he wasn't looking at me. But he was, I could tell. He was watching me sneakily, out of the corner of his eyes.

'OK then,' I said, 'if you're not interested—'

I let myself down into the pit and peered into the gap in the rock. I could see through! There was a big hollow space on the other side—maybe even a cave. I thought, I could squeeze through this gap.

I was excited now. There was a whole secret world down there. Even if I didn't find Hope Spring I had to go down, just to look around, see what it was like.

'I'm just going to have a quick look round. OK?' I told Chingwe.

It should have felt weird talking to an ape. But it didn't. Besides, I'd already decided that Chingwe was more human than some people I knew.

And he didn't call you a show-off.

The kitchen door was wide open. I jerked my thumb at it, 'Go back inside, Chingwe,' I told him. 'Go find Ma and Pa.'

Then I started wriggling, feet first, through the hole in the rock.

I was halfway through, flapping my feet around for footholds, when Chingwe started screeching his distress call. It was so shrill and panicky that I panicked too.

Oh no! I thought. What's wrong with him?

42

I hauled myself out of the hole, went scrambling up to the top of the pit.

Chingwe was dragging his leg around, like a wounded bird drags its wing. He was shrieking—it was horrible, it sounded so human: *'Eek, eek, eek eek!'*

At first I was really scared. I thought he'd hurt himself badly.

'Chingwe, come here, what you done?'

Then I saw his brown eyes. They were watching me, craftily, from under his craggy eyebrows.

I relaxed then; I started to grin with relief.

'Chingwe!' I scolded him. 'I know what you're trying to do!' It was like I could read his mind. 'There's nothing wrong with you, is there? You're trying to stop me going down that hole, aren't you? You think it's dangerous!'

I was touched. I really was. I gave Chingwe a big, matey smile.

'Good acting, Chingwe,' I told him. 'You should be in the Whirligig Theatre Company! But a bit over the top, don't you think? I know that trick, anyway. I seen you use it with Boss, remember? I'll be all right though. You don't need to worry about me. Honest.'

He stopped that terrible shrieking. He seemed to calm down a bit.

'Come on.' I led him by the hand back to the kitchen. I gave him a pink grapefruit to turn inside out.

'I won't be long,' I promised him. 'Be cool.'

I ducked out of the kitchen before he could make a scene. Then I ducked back. 'Just getting a torch,' I explained. I grabbed one from the kitchen shelf then slid out of the door.

But he shambled out after me, his chops all sticky with pink juice. For heaven's sake! I thought, exasperated. It was worse than towing a little brother round with you everywhere.

43

'All right,' I told Chingwe, 'just sit there and wait.' He squatted down by the pit. 'But don't make that screechy noise, right, when I go away!'

He shot me a quick, sideways look, then went back to shredding his grapefruit, peering at it, holding it close up to his face, as if he needed glasses.

Suddenly, I didn't want to leave him. I wasn't worried that Ma and Pa wouldn't look after him. I just wanted him with me. For a crazy second I thought about trying to take him with me. But I knew straight away that it was a cruel idea. Chingwe was a bag of nerves already. He'd spent his life locked in cramped, dark places when he should have been climbing in tree-tops.

You can't take him down there, I thought, looking into the dark hole. It's not fair—he'll go ape.

'OK, I'm going then,' I explained to him. 'I won't be long. I've got to find Hope Spring. It's urgent, see. If we don't have water, we'll have to leave Broom Cottage. We won't have a home any more.'

No screeching. He was too busy smacking his lips over his grapefruit. I breathed a sigh of relief and slithered down the hole.

Into a secret underground world. Into old limestone caves that could have been filled up with water for thousands, even millions of years.

Six

I lowered myself through the gap in the rock. All the time my ears were on red alert, waiting for Chingwe's shrieks. But he didn't make a sound.

Still, I couldn't help thinking, I hope he's OK. I almost went back to look.

I told myself, 'Stop worrying about him.'

I tried to forget about him, at least for a while, so I could concentrate on finding Hope Spring.

I was climbing down a shaft, where, for as long as I could remember, Hope Spring had bubbled up. It was easy climbing. The sides had split into great cracks like crazy paving. And tree roots looped their way through the cracks making natural hand and footholds.

I felt a little tingle, of fear and excitement. But otherwise, I was really pleased with how cool I was.

'No going bananas on this trip,' I said.

I felt a fool then, for talking out loud. As if those girls were checking up on me, even here underground.

I looked up. The sky looked down at me like a blue eye. Chingwe was somewhere up there, waiting for me.

Don't think about Chingwe. He'll be all right.

I lowered myself further down. The blue eye vanished. I was in darkness now—the shaft had gulped me in, like a throat.

I began to get scared.

'What did you come down here for?' I asked myself, clinging to the side of the shaft like a spider. 'Whose stupid idea was this anyway?'

One foot searched around for the next foothold. And found nothing. It waggled about in empty air.

'Oh, no!'

I was sliding down, scraping on rock walls. Desperately, I grabbed out for roots, rocks, anything to save myself. But I didn't slide far. *Whump*, I crash-landed on a nest of sticks.

It knocked me breathless. But I was still in one piece.

It wasn't totally dark down here, not pitch black. That surprised me. There were splashes of greyer blackness, where light trickled in. I squinted around me, trying to make things out.

What were those? Those hulking great shapes sneaking up on me?

I grabbed my torch out of my back pocket, clicked it on, swept it wildly about. The beam joggled all over the place because I was trembling so much.

'Prat,' I told myself.

Those dark shapes weren't subterranean monsters. I swept my torch around some more—the beam was steadier now.

'Wow!' I was in a cave—a proper cave.

And those shapes that had scared me were stalagmites. Great amber-coloured columns of them like melted toffee. They were sprouting out of the ground all around me like some kind of fantasy garden.

'Wow!' I was really impressed.

I flashed my torch over the roof. It sparkled with baby stalactites, crammed close together, like sharks' teeth.

I climbed off the pile of sticks and flicked my torch over it. Among the tree branches and stones were a busted football, a child's sandal. It was debris, swept here by the force of the water.

I expected to be splashing through water. But I wasn't, I was sliding on slippery mud. Whoever had pumped off Hope Spring had done a good job of it. They'd left nothing behind for anyone else. Just a few puddles on the floor.

Flashing my torch around again, I found what seemed

like a way forward. I didn't like the look of it though. It was a hole, like a jagged mouth, at the top of a great heap of rocks. The rocks looked as if they were made of sugar—they glistened ghostly-white in the torch light. I played my torch beam around the walls. There were some other holes and cracks and crevices. None that I could squeeze through.

So I scrambled up the rocks. A dribble of water leaked on to my head. I tasted it. It was clean and pure. It tasted of flowers. I was going the right way.

At the top of the rock pile I shoved my head into the tunnel mouth. I checked it out with my torch. It vanished into blackness, my torch beam couldn't find the end of it. But it didn't look bad. No worse than crawling through a giant water pipe. I hesitated for a second. I was thinking about Chingwe, eating his grapefruit, waiting patiently for me to come back. Then I pocketed my torch, hoisted myself in and started crawling.

I was blind as a mole in the dark. Except, even here, pale skinny fingers of light poked down from the surface. I was closed in by smooth walls. They were greasy and wet, like sweaty skin.

I felt cold, then sick. I couldn't see anything, couldn't hear anything. It was silent as a grave. Apart from the spooky drip, drip, drip of water coming through the limestone rock.

Then, suddenly, I couldn't move. A gut-chilling thought had frozen my muscles, locked them right up: *What if they let the water back in? While I'm stuck down here?*

No one knew I was down here—except Chingwe.

I couldn't believe I hadn't thought about it before. What if Ma had kicked ass at Aqua North: 'Give us our water back NOW or DIE!' What if they gave back Hope Spring, turned off the pump they'd used to steal it? Nightmarish pictures filled my mind—of water crashing through these tomblike tunnels. Gathering speed, making the ground thunder like

47

runaway horses. I'd hear it coming. But I'd be helpless. I wouldn't be fast enough. No way. It would come roaring along here with terrible force. Smash over me, carry me helplessly with it, gurgling into my nose, mouth, and down into my lungs. What if my body got carried up into the sunlight and Chingwe saw it? Chingwe's brain was messed up already. What would that do to him?

I couldn't breathe then. I was in a cold, sweating panic, curled up on the tunnel floor, fighting for breath, writhing around, choking, like I did in Spike's death scene.

And that's when I heard it: 'Tee hee hee.' I heard cold sneery voices whispering:

'He's getting really carried away.'

'Talk about over the top.'

'What?' I gasped.

'You heard.'

I gazed bewildered into the dark. As if I really expected those girls had crawled all the way down here just to mock me.

There was nobody there, of course. It was all in my head. No mocking eyes. No water booming through the tunnels either.

'Prat.' I was shivery and weak but at least I'd stopped panicking. I was back in control—just about.

'You nearly went bananas there,' I told myself sternly. 'Stop imagining all this crap about drowning. Right?'

I thought again about turning back. Chingwe might need me—I hadn't thought about him for at least thirty seconds. He must have finished his grapefruit by now—he'd be getting bored. I almost did turn back. Then I told myself, 'Nemo, don't you dare. You're using Chingwe as an excuse—because you're too scared to go on.' I decided that was feeble. I decided I had to keep on crawling.

And besides, I had to keep looking for Hope Spring. Track it back to where it was being stolen. Without our water supply all of us, Chingwe included, were in desperate trouble.

I dropped out at the end of the tunnel on to a sandy floor. I shone my torch upwards. I was in another cave, a massive one this time. My torch beam couldn't find the roof—it seemed as high as a cathedral. I flashed my torch on to the opposite wall.

A blaze of white fire nearly blinded me! I staggered back, shielding my eyes.

Something sprang out at me. Armed with terrible teeth, claws—

'Christ!' I dropped the torch, scrabbled for it on the floor, switched it on. The rock wall dazzled like diamonds—

I clean forgot about being cool, about not getting carried away.

For a full minute at least my mouth just hung open. Good job no one else was there, I looked like a total retard.

I closed my mouth, snap, and walked up for a closer inspection. I rubbed at the sparkling rock. I didn't need the torch because it glowed in the dark. But I shone the torch on it anyway.

'Phew!' That's all I could say, 'Phew!'

Then, at last, some words struggled out of my mouth.

'That's smart!' I said out loud. My voice echoed round the cave. It was excited, really over the top. But I just couldn't help it.

'That's the smartest, most incredible thing I've ever seen in my entire life!'

My voice went on echoing, 'Life, life, life . . . '

Seven

There was a dinosaur on the wall. Not all of him. Just his fossilized skeleton. It was pressed really neatly into the rock like a perfect pressed flower.

I floodlit him again with my torch. Then jumped back.

It almost seemed as if he was alive.

'Don't be stupid,' I told myself. 'He's just bones.'

And his bones glittered because they were coated with white crystals. They looked like sugar. But they were calcite crystals, precipitated out of the spring water.

'I can't believe you!' I shook my head at the dinosaur in the rock. I turned my torch off and let him glow softly like a luminous watch.

It was a brilliant discovery. I felt like shouting it to the world. But there was nobody here to share it with me. Only me, on my own, in the dark.

I almost wished I'd made Chingwe come with me, so he could see it too. He'd be really bowled over! I could imagine his hoots of surprise, 'Ooo, ooo, ooo.' How he'd shuffle up close to the rock, squint at it from about ten centimetres away, poke at it, give it a really good sniff . . .

'You're unbelievable!' I told the fossil dinosaur. I was really thrilled with him—he was beautiful.

He reared up on long hind legs, balanced on a thin, bony tail. His clawed hands reached out like grappling hooks ready to grip and tear. His skull looked frail and delicate. But it was cramful of killer teeth, like tiny curved knives. And his mouth was wide open, as if he was going to roar.

He wasn't big. He was a sort of pocket dinosaur, only a

metre tall. But, don't get me wrong, he wasn't cute. He was deadly.

'He's a little raptor,' I decided. 'Maybe Compsognathus.'

Once, I'd been dinosaur crazy, a bit of an expert. I'd collected models, knew all their names, read every dinosaur book I could get my hands on. I'd seen loads of photos of fossil dinosaurs, even crystallized ones like this—that's how I knew that the white, sugary stuff was calcite. But often the pictures I'd seen were just jumbles of bones. Palaeontologists had to fit them together like jigsaws.

But this sparkling fossil was perfect, better than anything I'd seen in any book. His toes were perfect. That slashing claw that folded up when they were sprinting—even that was there.

'Nemo, you've found something really special,' I whispered to myself.

Suddenly, I felt myself shivering. Good job he's not alive, I thought. I wouldn't like to meet him, down here, on my own, in these dark caves.

He'd sniff you out. Spring at you feet first. Rip your guts out with one kick. And don't even think of outrunning him. You wouldn't stand a chance. He could move like greased lightning.

I switched on the torch. What's that? I thought, going nearer.

The crystals made his bones stand out really clearly, like looking at a glowing X-ray. But all round his skeleton were fuzzier marks. I didn't have a clue what they were. I peered at them up close, traced the outline with my fingers.

'They're ferns,' I decided.

They looked like fern leaves, pressed into the rock. As if the raptor was lying on a bed of ferns when it died.

The torch beam started flickering.

Oh no! I thought. The batteries are packing up! I shook the torch. It stopped flickering—it seemed OK.

But it made me remember why I was down in the caves. It had nothing to do with fossil raptors. I was supposed to be tracking Hope Spring. And Chingwe was waiting for me above ground—I'd promised him not to be long. He'd be getting restless. I couldn't afford to waste any more time.

I played my torch round the walls.

Oh great! I thought.

I'd found the place where the water came in. It was a great slash in the rock above me.

There's no way I can get up there, I thought.

There was only a dribble of water now. But when Hope Spring flowed through it must be a gushing waterfall, crashing down to the cave floor.

I went over and put my cupped hands under the dribble. Then I sipped some of the water. It was Hope Spring all right.

But it was the end of the road. I'd need climbing gear to get up there. There were no easy handholds in the smooth, slippery rock. I couldn't track Hope Spring back any further. Now I'd never find out where Aqua North were tapping it off.

'Better go home,' I sighed, disappointed.

I took one last look at Compsognathus. That cheered me up. It was a great find, a really brilliant find. I couldn't wait to get back and tell everyone all about it.

I was just going to start the return journey. I was already thinking how pleased Chingwe would be when he saw me, how he'd whoop a welcome, 'Hoo, hoo, hoo!' in his funny, high-pitched voice, when I felt the air rippling over my head. Something fluttery swooped into my hair.

'Aaagh, aaagh!!' I hollered, flapping my arms around my head.

My yells went booming around the cave, made my head buzz. Then the echoes faded away . . . There was dead silence, except for the drip, drip, drip of the water.

I stopped dancing about. I felt a bit of a prat. I patted my hair. Nothing there.

'For heaven's sake,' I told myself. 'It's probably just bats! There's always bats in caves.'

But I gripped my torch a lot more tightly.

'You nearly went bananas just then,' I told myself angrily. 'The torch nearly flew out your hand. Then you'd have been in big trouble.'

I took a step. Something rustled. Flinching, I shone the torch at the floor.

'Where'd that come from?'

It was a book.

I poked it with my foot. Then I picked it up. The pages fluttered like bats' wings. I gazed upwards.

It came from up there, I thought. That's what hit me on the head.

I inspected the book, shone my torch on it. It was a drawing book from W.H. Smith. It wasn't old or anything. It could have been bought yesterday. What was it doing here, in these ancient caves?

More and more puzzled, I flicked through it. It was full of pencil drawings.

They were drawings of wildlife, birds of prey mainly—kestrels, merlins, buzzards—swooping over a rocky landscape. They were pretty good, I could tell that because I'm a bit of an artist myself. But this stuff was way out of my league. Some of the drawings were anatomical, like the ones you get in biology textbooks. There was a wing spread out and every detail, every barb in every feather carefully drawn in. Whoever drew these knew how hawks worked.

I flicked to another page. There was a drawing of a hawk's skull. It wasn't gross or anything. It was really clever. The skull looked fragile, delicate, as if it was made out of eggshell.

I closed the book, shone my torch upwards.

'Hello!' I shouted.

Straight away I felt like a fool. How could there be anyone, up there in the dark?

For a start, there was no way up there.

I swung the torch around. Yes, there was. The torch highlighted Compsognathus, a giant stalagmite like a melted candle, then a limestone staircase . . .

'Check that out, Nemo,' I told myself.

I swung the torch back. Heaped high against the cave wall was a natural staircase, made out of big limestone blocks. It disappeared into the dark, like the grand staircase to some ruined castle.

I started to climb it, with the torch in one hand, the sketch book in another. I didn't feel very scared—that surprised me. I felt curious mostly. I wanted to see who'd made these drawings. I was sure that, whoever it was, they'd want this book back. If it were mine, it would be a precious possession.

I climbed higher and higher, until the staircase ran out and there was nowhere else to go. I could almost touch the cave roof now. I was very close to the surface—there were tree roots coming through, dangling like giant worms.

I stood on the last limestone block wondering what to do next. 'Hello,' I said, as an experiment. I was 99.9 per cent certain no one would answer.

'Hello,' a muffled voice answered, next to my ear.

Shocked, I spun round, almost tumbled right off that grand staircase.

There was no one behind me. The cave wall seemed dark and solid, like rock. But when I shone the torch on it I saw there was no wall at all, just a tangle of roots. And between some of them, I could see blue sky.

'Where are you?' came the voice again.

'I'm here,' I said. Then I thought how stupid that sounded. 'I'm under the ground,' I explained. 'In a cave.'

'Are you stuck?' called the voice.

And then I had another shock. A hand came snaking through the roots. It felt about, touched my face.

'Is that you?'

'Yes!'

'Oh, right. Sorry.'

The hand wriggled back.

I thought, This is unbelievable! I mean, I've got a crazy imagination. But even I couldn't have dreamed up something like this.

I pressed my face close to the tangled root ball. There was a slit of light, where the hand had come in. I peered through. It felt like being inside a postbox, looking out.

Then I shrank back. I was staring straight into two blue eyes.

'Is this your sketch book?' I said, holding the book up, trying to show it to the blue eyes.

'Oh yes,' came the voice. 'It fell through a crack in the rock.'

I even tried pushing the sketch book through the tiny gap to the outside. It wouldn't fit.

'Wait a minute,' the voice said. 'Mind your face.'

I reeled back, 'Hey!' A wicked-looking combat knife slid in through the roots. It started to chop about, making the gap bigger.

'Hey!' I yelled. 'What you doing?'

'Trying . . . to . . . get . . . you . . . out,' came the breathless voice from outside.

'I'm not actually trapped down here, you know!' I yelled. 'I don't need rescuing. There's a way out. How d'you think I got in here!'

But the blade carried on slicing away at the roots. It was fast, effective. It was razor sharp. Whoever was using it knew how to handle a knife.

'Can you get out now?'

'I think so.'

I dragged myself through the hacked-off roots. Out of the dark cave—into fresh air and wind and sunshine.

Eight

'Be careful,' I warned myself. I was instantly wary. Not because of that wicked knife. But because of the girl who was holding it.

She put the knife down. It didn't make me feel any safer.

I was already thinking of ways to escape. I told myself, 'You've got to get back to Chingwe. He'll be fed up with waiting by now. He'll be really worried—'

'Hi,' the girl said, springing forward.

I sprang back, nearly tripped over a rock. 'Calm down. Be cool,' I told myself.

'I'm Martha,' the girl said. She stuck her hand out. Come on! Surely I wasn't supposed to shake it?

By now there were frantic alarm bells clanging inside my brain. What's she so friendly for? I've only just met her. She's really over-the-top.

'Hi,' I muttered, reluctantly. 'I'm Nemo.'

I'm not a shy person. How could I be? I was raised in the Whirligig Theatre Company. I'm the extrovert type, a natural-born showman. Ma says, 'Nemo, you could talk the hind leg off a donkey.'

But Martha made me feel tongue-tied. Like a shrinking violet! Ma wouldn't have believed it. I could hardly believe it myself.

'Er, er . . . ' I mumbled, shoving her sketch book at her.

There were eager words bubbling up in my throat, like, 'Those pictures are class. They're brilliant—I wish I could draw hawks like that.' But I gulped them back down again. 'Be cool!' I warned myself, desperately. 'Don't make a fool of yourself. Just BE COOL.'

'Thanks,' Martha said. She seemed wary herself now, not so friendly as she was before.

We watched each other.

She was tall, as tall as I was, with long brown hair. She was wearing a baggy check shirt and jeans and trainers with no socks or laces. There was a pencil stuck behind her ear— a yellow pencil with black rings round it. And she had a little scar shaped like a new moon above her left eyebrow. I only noticed it because it was light pink, worm-coloured, and the rest of her face was tanned.

I glanced at the combat knife shining in the grass. I thought, Maybe she uses that knife to sharpen her pencils.

The silence was getting awkward. She was rubbing the scar on her forehead, as if it hurt. But it couldn't have done because it was an old scar.

My brain was a mess, overloaded with strange new feelings—shyness, embarrassment, stuff like that. I was a nervous wreck, as bad as Chingwe. What was happening to me? It was really cramping my style. I didn't know how to behave with people any more. Especially with girls.

My eyes flickered about. I tried to unscramble my brain, tried to think of some lie—so I could make a quick getaway. I had to lie, didn't I? I could hardly say, 'Chingwe—he's an ape, probably a humanzee actually—is sitting waiting for me to come up from underground. And he gets in a state, he's very easily upset. So I've got to hurry away now. Bye!' How could I say the truth? She'd think I was a nutter, an escaped lunatic . . .

Then I realized that, even if I made up a lie, I couldn't go anywhere. Because I didn't know where I was.

My eyes flickered around a bit more. There were no landmarks I recognized.

'Where am I ?' I said, thinking out loud, staring at all the unfamiliar rocks and trees.

Then I thought, cringing, Oh no, why did I say that? She'll think I'm a dickhead, getting lost!

I was forced to explain a bit more, so she didn't think I was a complete idiot. I felt awkward. I was even blushing. I could feel my ear lobes going pink. Me, Nemo, blushing!

'I . . . I . . . I live in Broom Cottage,' I stammered at her. 'I don't get lost, not usually. But I've been down there, underground.' I stamped my foot on the rock, it made a hollow booming sound, like a drum. 'I must have come further than I thought.'

She was staring at me. But it totally surprised me—because she didn't look scornful or sneering, like she'd been having a good laugh at my expense.

Instead she seemed really interested. She started to ask me loads of questions: 'There are caves down there, aren't there? Are there stalagmites and things? What's it like?'

She seemed genuinely keen to know. I could have blurted out, 'I found this amazing fossil raptor!' and raved on about it for ten, fifteen minutes. I could have got all over-excited, carried away with enthusiasm. The old Nemo would've done that, no question. But the new Nemo wasn't so dumb. He was a lot smarter.

'Tell me about it then,' she said. 'It must have been great!'

But I just shrugged, kept my voice flat as a ruler. 'Naa,' I gave an even bigger shrug. 'Naa. Nothing to tell. Dead boring.'

I was pleased with the way the new Nemo sounded. He sounded cooler than cool.

Only Martha wasn't impressed. She shot me this look that was half-pitying, half-disappointed. Then she shrugged too, as if I was a lost cause or something.

I thought, What's the matter with her? I was really confused—I couldn't work out what I'd done wrong. I was well cool. I'd got everything under control. So what was she looking at me like that for?

But there was no time to work it out. 'Martha!' someone called faintly from what seemed like a long way off. 'Martha!'

Martha picked up her knife, slid it into a leather sheath on her belt.

'That's my mum shouting me,' she said. 'I've got to go home now.'

I should have thought, Good! I should have gone back to Chingwe. But she'd got me curious, I just couldn't help it. Where did she get that wicked-looking combat knife? Shops don't sell those to kids. How does she know so much about hawks? Where did she get a hawk skeleton? Did she bury a dead hawk? Then dig it up when the maggots had picked it clean? My brain was fizzing with questions. She wasn't like any girl I'd ever known. But I couldn't ask her anything, could I? Being nosy just isn't cool.

'Bye,' she said. 'See you sometime. Thanks for my sketch book.'

I watched her climb along a ravine, through a cleft in the rock. Any second now I'd lose sight of her, maybe never see her again . . .

'But I don't know where I am!' I yelled after her.

I could've kicked myself. I sounded so lost and helpless, like a pathetic little kid. I thought, She'll think you're a wimp now. She'll laugh at you!

But when she turned round she wasn't laughing at me. She just looked concerned. When she puckered up her forehead, the new moon scar didn't pucker at all, it stayed smooth—I don't know why I especially noticed that.

She came back and said, 'I'll show you the way to Broom Cottage. It's not far. But first I need to tell Mum where we're going.'

I didn't move. I was confused again. I didn't know what I was supposed to do.

'Come on then,' she said.

So I followed her through the bone-dry hills.

She was chatty again. 'We're your nearest neighbours,' she told me.

I frowned. Neighbours? I was thinking. I didn't know we had any neighbours.

''Course,' she went on, 'you probably don't know a lot about us. We're the le Dukes. We haven't been here that long. It's great here, isn't it? Dad says it's the perfect place to prepare for Armageddon.'

I had to break my silence, I just couldn't help it. 'What?' I said, louder than I intended. 'Did you just say *Armageddon*?'

But she was too far ahead to hear me. I thought, Naa, she can't have said that. My ears must be playing tricks.

She was a really good climber—I had to hurry to keep up with her. When I crossed a dried-up stream bed, she was waiting for me on the other side.

'That's where I live,' she said, pointing.

That did it. I cracked. 'Wow!' I said. 'Wow!' My coolness fell off, just fell off, like an ice overcoat. I fired questions at her like a machine gun. 'Where'd that place come from? Who built it? How long has it been there?'

Once, Ma had to wear a corset, to get into this Victorian dress. Ma's skinny, right, but this dress had a waist that was twenty-two inches, it was for a stick insect! So, Pa laced her into this Victorian corset before the show and afterwards, when Ma got unlaced she said, 'Phew! What a relief. I can take big breaths again!' And that's just what I felt like when those questions came bursting out of my mouth. Like Ma, being unlaced from her corset.

'Who built it?' I asked Martha again.

'Dad built it,' said Martha, sounding proud. 'He put a call out on the Net—'

'You on the Internet?' I got surprised all over again. I don't know why, lots of people are on the Net. But somehow

61

it didn't fit with that primitive-looking knife she carried and her pencil drawings of bones.

''Course we are. Anyhow, some people came and helped Dad. But he did lots of the work himself. There was nothing here before we came, nothing at all, just some broken-down buildings.'

I remembered those crumbling old buildings. I knew where I was now. I could have found my way back to Broom Cottage and Chingwe, no problem. I shouldn't have left him waiting so long. And Ma and Pa would be worried sick about Hope Spring. I should have been back there . . .

But instead I said, 'Wow!' again. 'I can't believe this,' I told her.

I was staring at somebody's private kingdom. It seemed to have sprung up from nowhere—a house and lots of outbuildings and land, protected by a high, wire fence. There were fuel tanks inside the fence, vehicles, wind turbines, even a JCB.

But what was really amazing, much more than all this, was that the grass was green. I swear it, the grass inside that fence was green. Green grassy meadows—they were the kind of thing that only existed in fairy stories. But I was standing there looking at them. Sheep were grazing on the juicy grass inside the fence.

'You've got water!' I marvelled.

'We're lucky,' said Martha. 'We've got our own private supply.'

'We did too,' I told her. 'It was called Hope Spring. But Aqua North stole it. They're crooks, they are! My Ma and Pa are trying to get it back. We can't live here without it. Me and Ma and Pa and—' I was going to add Chingwe but then I thought of all the explaining I'd have to do. So I just said, 'We'd all have to move away.'

She seemed really shocked. She said, 'That's terrible. You mean, they just took your water? Ask my dad—he'll let you

62

have some of ours until you get yours back. I mean, we're neighbours. And good neighbours help each other out, don't they?'

I didn't know how to answer that. I felt a bit ashamed. Whirligig Theatre Company were lousy neighbours. We were always on the road for a start. And when we did come home we kept ourselves to ourselves.

So I just said, 'Ma and Pa'll be really grateful—'

We skidded down a rocky slope and Martha led me into the compound. I noticed that the fence was electric, like the one Dr Dekler switched off at the Primate Rehabilitation Centre. I wondered, What do they need an electric fence for? Out here, in the middle of nowhere?

But there wasn't time to give it any more thought. Because we were inside Martha's house.

I was prepared for anything. I thought nothing else could surprise me. Except the cosy scene that I found there. Martha's mum was sitting at the kitchen table. She had a long, flowery dress on and little girls crowding round her like a flock of birds. She was telling them a story.

I've always been a sucker for story-telling, ever since I was small. So I couldn't help listening in.

Martha's mum had a Bible open in front of her. But she didn't need it because she knew this story by heart. She was telling the little kids about Noah and the Great Flood. How mankind had got really wicked. So God sent this Great Flood to destroy them and every living thing on the planet. Except for Noah, who was a good man. So God told Noah to build an ark and fill it with two of every kind of animal. And, when the Great Flood came, Noah and his family were saved.

'And all the animals were saved,' Martha's mum told the children. 'See our sheep out there? See those big crows in our trees? Their great, great, great, great, great, great grandmas and grandads were with Noah on the ark.'

I couldn't help grinning at those little kids' faces. Their eyes were wide and starry, their mouths made round 'O' shapes. When Whirligig Theatre Company did a show, the little kids in the audience looked just like that.

The story had props—that made me like it even more. There was a beautiful wooden ark on the table—it looked as if it was hand-carved. It had elephants, giraffes, monkeys, every kind of creature. 'Look,' said Martha's mum, picking up a wooden chimpanzee. 'He went into the ark with Noah too.' And she made the toy monkey jump up the gangplank, into the ark.

I thought about Chingwe back home, waiting. But not for long because Mrs le Duke looked up and saw us and smiled. She had a magical smile. It made me feel warm and safe and peaceful inside, as if I was one of those little kids gathering round her, listening to her story.

She's a really nice mum, I thought. I decided that instantly. She's a proper mum. Not crazy like my ma. I conveniently forgot how my crazy ma let me keep Chingwe. Instead I felt jealous of Martha, having a nice, *normal* mum, like I imagined all other kids had.

Martha introduced me. 'This is Nemo, Mum. He comes from Broom Cottage. This is my mum, Nemo, and all my little sisters.'

I flashed Martha's mum my best smile. Ma says I can charm the birds off the trees if I want to. I wanted to charm Mrs le Duke—I wanted her to approve of me. It seemed really important.

'Pleased to meet you, Nemo,' said Mrs le Duke with a friendly smile back.

A shadow fell across me. I turned around. There was someone in the doorway.

'And this is my dad,' said Martha.

A man in his work clothes came into the kitchen. He had to stoop to get through the doorway. He had muddy jeans on, a black T-shirt, and heavy steel-capped boots.

Martha's dad was a big, powerful man—he seemed to fill up the room. He was much taller and stronger than my little pa. Much, much stronger. He could lift up my pa with one hand! He was like Iron Man. I could see his iron muscles.

He had a black beard, like a prophet out of the Bible. And the most startling blue eyes I'd ever seen. Those eyes were looking straight at me.

'Hello, Mr le Duke,' I said, keeping my voice very polite and respectful. I couldn't seem to look away from those eyes.

It's like they were hypnotizing me. They were blazing with truth and honesty. They were like blue fire, like blue ice. Mr le Duke didn't seem to need to blink them.

He didn't need to speak either. Not until he felt good and ready. At last he nodded and said, 'Hello, son.'

'This is Nemo, Dad. He's our neighbour.'

'Welcome, neighbour,' said Mr le Duke, in his deep, slow-talking voice.

He was super-cool, without even trying! He was like a film hero—the tough, silent one who doesn't waste words.

But what he'd said, 'Welcome, neighbour,' made me feel tickled pink. Like I'd somehow been accepted and approved of.

Mr le Duke opened a door—I caught a glimpse of a PC and some other computer gear on a desk. Then he went inside and shut the door behind him. Without him the kitchen seemed empty, even though it was still full of people.

The little girls started chattering again. I suddenly realized they'd been awfully quiet while their dad had been in the room. As quiet as mice.

Martha said, 'I won't be long, Mum. I'll just show Nemo the way home.'

'Did you get lost, son?' asked Mrs le Duke, smiling that lovely, peaceful smile.

'I was underground,' I explained, 'in the caves. I don't usually get lost.'

'Those caves are confusing,' she sympathized. 'My husband says so.'

'Has he been down there?' I asked her, surprised.

'Oh yes. He was very glad to find them. He says they're perfect for storage.'

I nodded politely at her, as if I knew what she meant. I wanted to ask her, 'Did he find Hope Spring? Did he see Compsognathus?' I hadn't told a soul about Compsognathus yet—I hadn't had a chance. I might have told her—about Compsognathus, even about Chingwe. She was that kind of person; the kind you feel you can talk to, even though you've only just met them. Except that Martha was already on her way out of the door.

'You come and visit us whenever you like, son,' said Mrs le Duke. 'We welcome neighbours anytime! I'll bake some peanut butter cookies for you.'

I felt really grateful, as if she'd given me a big present. And when I said, 'I'll look forward to that, Mrs le Duke,' I meant it with all my heart.

As I turned to follow Martha, I tried to think of something I could give in return. I thought, Perhaps the little girls would like Chingwe. Perhaps they'd like to play with him.

But I knew straight away that could never happen. Chingwe wasn't a cuddly, trained chimp in an advert. You couldn't trust Chingwe with people. He'd been hurt by them too much in the past. He might nip the little girls, even chuck stones at them.

I thought, He'll probably nip *me* when I get back. Probably throw one of his screaming tantrums or something.

I hadn't meant to stay away for so long. Suddenly, I felt really uneasy. Searching for Hope Spring, finding Compsognathus, meeting Martha and her family—our new neighbours. So much had happened. Chingwe had got pushed to the back of my mind. Was he still crouching by the empty pit, with that worried frown on his face? Waiting for me to come back, like I promised?

I didn't want to let Chingwe down. He'd been let down by people all his life.

'Naa,' I reassured myself. 'He won't be still waiting. He'll have got bored by now—or hungry. He'll have gone back to pester Ma and Pa in the house.'

He was probably in the house now, turning a pink grapefruit inside-out, slurping the juice. He liked doing that. That made him happy.

I hurried after Martha towards the gate. On my way, I snatched a grass stem and chewed it. The le Duke grass was sappy and sweet. Not like the dry, shrivelled stuff on everyone else's land.

How do they do it? I thought.

Outside the fence, I turned for a last look back at the le Duke property.

Something was glinting at the back of their house. It reflected the sun like a silver mirror.

What's that? I thought, screwing my eyes up.

But then a cloud came over and whatever it was stopped shining.

'Wait for me!' I yelled. I wiped the sweat off my forehead and followed Martha over the baking-hot limestone.

Nine

'That's a kestrel,' said Martha, looking up and shading her eyes against the sun.

She slung her long brown hair back over her shoulder so she could see better. She had a savage knife in her belt and a scar on her forehead and a pencil behind her ear and a drawing book in her hand. She looked like a warrior princess—who likes sketching.

I was glad I'd yelled after her, 'I don't know where I am!' even though it made me feel like a prat. If I hadn't stopped her, I'd probably never have seen her again, or met her family. It's lonely sometimes, being in the Whirligig Theatre Company. It's lonely on the road. I never stay in any school long. I never get the chance to make proper friends or go round to their houses.

'Do you know,' my new friend told me, 'that mouse pee glows in ultra-violet light?'

'Pardon?' I said. I'd been lost in my thoughts. I still felt warm, tingly all over, from the le Duke family's welcome. In between worrying about Chingwe, I kept thinking about them. I'd been mixed-up lately, since I played Spike's death scene. I'd been full of confusion and doubt. But Martha's mum and dad were wise, strong people—I felt that as soon as I met them. Especially her dad. You couldn't imagine *him* having doubts, not being sure of himself. There was no doubt in his blue eyes at all.

'Mouse pee glows in ultra-violet light and kestrels can see ultra-violet light,' Martha explained. 'So when a kestrel sees a trail of glowing pee it thinks, Dinner time! and it comes zooming down.'

'Oh, right!' I said. 'How do you know stuff like that?'

'I learned it. I'm going to be a biologist,' she said. She sounded really excited about that. 'Dad says it's a good thing to be.'

'Oh, right,' I nodded. I thought, I'd like to take some career advice from Mr le Duke. Once, being on the road with the Whirligig Theatre Company, doing their shows, was all that I wanted. Now I didn't know what I wanted any more.

Together, in blinding sunshine, we struggled up a crumbling, rocky slope. It was hot, hard work. But soon, we'd be able to see Broom Cottage.

I felt a bit more relaxed with Martha, not on my guard every second. But I was still watching my mouth. I didn't want it to flap too much. Better to be strong and silent, like Mr le Duke.

But I couldn't help asking, 'What school do you go to?'

'I don't go to school.' Martha stopped at the top of the slope and waited for me to catch up with her.

'You're kidding!' I said amazed soon as I got my breath back. My mouth started babbling again—questions poured out of it. 'Where do you learn biology stuff from then? Do you watch wildlife films on telly? Do you—'

'We haven't got a telly,' she interrupted me.

'No telly!' This time I didn't have to worry about my mouth flapping. I was struck dumb.

'No. I learn things from Mum and Dad. They teach us at home. And I learn from watching animals and drawing them. And from books. We've got lots of American books. Mum and Dad send away specially for them. They say American books are the best.'

I didn't know about American books but I took it for granted that Mrs and Mr le Duke must be right. 'So I bet you're an expert on biology by now—with all these books,' I told Martha.

She didn't answer straight away. A sort of cloudy,

69

doubtful look passed over her face. Then she said a really strange thing, as if she was thinking out loud: 'Well, I *thought* I was,' she said.

She hesitated, seemed to make up her mind, then took something out of the back pocket of her jeans. I couldn't see what it was, her fingers were folded over it. 'I found this queer stone-thing in the dried-up bed of a stream,' she told me. 'I want you to tell me what it is.'

She started unfolding her hand just as I heard Chingwe's voice, floating over the hills. 'Hoo, hoo, hoo!'

I started yelling, at the top of my voice, 'Hey, Chingwe!'

Startled, Martha dropped the stone back into her pocket. 'I'll go home then,' she said, quickly.

And she was already on her way when, without thinking, I put out a hand to stop her. 'No,' I said. I realized I didn't want her to go. 'No, come and meet my ma. Come and meet Chingwe.'

'Who's Chingwe?'

'You'll see,' I grinned at her. 'Come on.'

Then, suddenly I wasn't relaxed any more. I felt dead nervous. I thought, Why did you ask her to stay? What's she going to think?

I wasn't worried about her meeting Chingwe. Chingwe was—just Chingwe. He couldn't help how he behaved. I was worried about her meeting Ma. I was already squirming with embarrassment just thinking about it.

I'd better explain about Ma. There isn't that safe feeling around her—not like you got around Mrs le Duke. Ma's not safe, she's unpredictable. You never know what she's going to say and do next. She really keeps you on your toes. Plus she looks weird. As we ran down to meet her I'd forgotten how weird Ma looks. Compared to a nice, flowery, story-telling, cookie-baking mum like Mrs le Duke.

Ma was in the back yard with Chingwe. They were staring into the dusty pit. As if they were wishing. As if, by wishing hard enough, they could make Hope Spring come bubbling up.

Oh no! I thought. Ma's got those stripy leggings on. Her legs look like two sticks of rock.

Ma's hair was like it usually is—bleached white and spiky. She'd had it like that as long as I could remember. But today, she had her purple knee-high Doc Martens on.

'What did she have to wear those for?' I groaned, cringing inside.

It got worse and worse because, as we got closer, I saw Ma's diamond nose stud and, on her arm, the tattoo of a dove with a leafy branch in its beak. I shook my head in despair. I'd forgotten about the tattoo and the nose stud—I mean, I'd got used to them. I didn't notice them any more. But I was *sure* Martha would notice them.

I was wrong though, because she wasn't even looking at Ma. She was staring at Chingwe. He was shambling along behind Ma with his old, grey towel (the one he used as a comfort blanket) in his fist. He was showing his gappy yellow teeth, stretching his lips back over his pink gums. It could have been a snarl—or a grin.

'Hey, Chingwe!' I greeted him, holding my arms out wide.

I wouldn't have blamed him if he'd been mad. In fact I was ready to duck because you never knew with Chingwe. He could have chucked something at me—some mud or a grapefruit skin or a pebble. He didn't care; he was like a delinquent grandad. Sometimes, he whirled his arms like windmills and *pretended* to chuck something. Then he laughed like a drain—these sort of snorting explosions— when you ducked for nothing. I wondered about Chingwe's sense of humour. Did other apes have a sense of humour— or only humanzees?

But this time, I didn't need to duck. Because Chingwe seemed pleased to see me. He came hurrying up to me.

71

'Sorry I was so long,' I told him. 'I never meant to be. It was just that, well, stuff kept happening.'

Chingwe peered at me with his sad old eyes. 'Hoo, hoo, hoo,' he moaned, as if he was telling me off. Then he squatted down. I squatted down too. He started to search my hair for nits—or maybe juggling fleas.

Meanwhile, Martha was still staring at him. She was pop-eyed! She shook her head as if she was dreaming.

'That's an ape!' she said, pointing a shaky finger. 'That's a real live ape!'

She knew her biology. She knew Chingwe wasn't a monkey. And she knew straight away that there was something special about him.

'Is he a chimp?' she asked me. 'He doesn't look like the ones in my books. He's walking upright!'

She didn't wait for an answer. She went bounding up to Ma. She wasn't at all shy with strangers—I used to be like that, once.

'Hello, how are you?' she greeted Ma.

Ma didn't answer her straight off. 'Who's this then, Nemo?' she said turning to me.

A twist of anxiety grabbed my guts. Was Ma going to be rude? She wasn't a serene type of person like Mrs le Duke. She could be really prickly sometimes, even spiteful. Especially when she was tired and worried. And she was both of those now. There were black stains under her eyes. I wondered if she'd managed to snatch any sleep.

'It's Martha,' I told her in a bright chirpy voice. 'She's our neighbour.'

'Hello, Martha.'

I breathed a sigh of relief. It was all right. Ma was being polite.

'Where's Pa gone?' I asked her. I'd suddenly noticed that the van wasn't there.

'He's gone to give that water company hell,' said Ma, narrowing her tired eyes.

I couldn't help raising my eyebrows. I couldn't imagine Pa giving anyone hell. He was too meek and mild. I thought about Mr le Duke. What if he went striding into Aqua North's HQ? They wouldn't give him the runaround—they wouldn't dare! They'd stand to attention, say, 'Yes, *sir*! Right away, *sir*! We'll give you your water back immediately, *sir*!'

'And I hope he brings back some emergency water supplies,' added Ma. 'All we've got is some bottles of tonic water.'

I opened my mouth to say, 'I know where you can get water.' But then I remembered that I hadn't asked Mr le Duke's permission like I ought to have done.

I thought, I'll just have to go back and ask him. But that was OK. I was looking for a reason to go back.

Martha was fascinated by Chingwe. She was sitting on the ground watching him. She'd hunched herself up, just like him, and she was gazing, with serious concentration, into his wrinkly face.

Like I said before, sometimes Chingwe looked all ape. But he looked quite human today. That little coconut head and skinny limbs—he looked like a hairy urchin child.

Chingwe was staring back at Martha. There was absolutely no expression on his face. With one hand he was scratching his belly. But I saw his other hand reach behind him and close on a stone.

Ma had seen it too. She warned me, 'Nemo, he's got a stone.'

'Chingwe!' I said. 'Don't you dare throw that!'

I apologized to Martha, 'Sorry, he's a bit of a hooligan. But he can't help it. It's 'cos he's scared of people.' I shrugged. 'And he's scared of other apes too.'

Gently, I unclasped Chingwe's fingers one by one and

took the stone away. Like an octopus he sneaked out another long arm. I thought he'd picked up another stone. His arm whirled round. 'Duck!' I yelled to Martha.

She didn't duck, she was too surprised. But nothing hit her. Confused, I looked back at Chingwe.

His shoulders were shaking with silent laughter. I opened his hand. It was empty.

'Sorry,' I told Martha, shrugging. 'It's his idea of a joke. Chingwe,' I said, wagging my finger at him, 'behave yourself.'

His arm snaked out again towards Martha's face and I thought, What's he going to do now? But he just gently traced the scar on her forehead with his fingernail and made hooting sounds like he was sad that she'd been injured. 'Don't,' I told him.

But Martha shrugged and said, 'It's OK.'

Martha squatted back on her heels. I thought she would give up on Chingwe. People don't like chimps who throw stones, or even pretend to. They don't like chimps who poke their scars. They like chimps to be clingy and cuddly and cute.

But Martha seemed even more interested. 'Where'd you get him?' she asked.

'In a freak show,' said Ma, before I could answer. She still sounded full of outrage about it. 'This idiot man had him cooped up in this tiny cage and was showing him as a humanzee. And he had the bare-faced cheek to say he wasn't being cruel. I ask you!'

'What's a humanzee?' said Martha.

I leapt in, eager to explain. 'You know, half chimpanzee, half human. Humanzee, get it? Like, the missing link. This scientist guy, Dr Dekler, at the Primate Rehabilitation place, he said Chingwe might be really important. He might be a living missing link—you know, that shows how people are descended from apes.'

I don't know how I expected Martha to react. But I didn't expect her to do what she did. She threw back her head and laughed out loud.

I was really startled. I mean, what was so funny about it? It was such a weird laugh too—sort of amazed and shocked and disbelieving. I laughed like that when I was a little kid and Ma first told me about sex. I just didn't believe it. I threw back my head and roared and said, 'Come on! You and Pa don't do *that*, do you?'

Martha was still grinning. 'People aren't descended from apes. Stop kidding me!'

She looked at Chingwe again. His brown eyes looked back at her, thoughtfully. Martha frowned. You could practically see her brain whizzing around. Then she turned on me. 'Stop kidding me!' she said again. She sounded really angry. 'Do you think I'm stupid or something?'

I was really bewildered. I couldn't understand why she was mad at me. I thought, frantically, What have I done wrong now? What have I said? Just when I thought we were getting along great. Just when I was really beginning to like her.

'But it's evolution, isn't it?' I appealed to her, desperately. 'All kids know about evolution! About how these fishy creatures crawled out of the swamps and changed into land creatures, like dinosaurs. Except that the dinosaurs died out, of course, and then, millions of years after that, we evolved from chimps and—'

'What's a dinosaur?' asked Martha.

You could've knocked me down with a feather. I was truly gobsmacked. I thought, I can't have heard right!

I said, 'Did you just say, *"What's a dinosaur?"*?'

'That's right,' she said. 'I don't know what that word means.'

'But all kids know about dinosaurs!' I was too amazed to be polite. 'You've got to be stupid not to know about dinosaurs!'

Her reaction was scary. She went ape.

'What are you telling me all this stupid rubbish for?' she screamed at me.

'Hoo, hoo, hoo!' Chingwe hooted with his fear-grin on his face. He was getting upset. He hated loud noises, especially shouting and rows.

'All what stupid rubbish?' I said, totally stunned. 'What you talking about?'

'All this stupid rubbish about people coming from chimps! From *that*!' she said, pointing at Chingwe. 'It's ridiculous!'

'Hey, wait a minute,' I said, insulted. 'Chingwe's more human than some people I know! And anyway,' I told her, 'Dr Dekler said chimps are our closest living relatives! Didn't he, Ma? You heard him? Didn't you, Ma?'

I turned to Ma for support. But she'd wandered off, in a world of her own. She was looking out over the hills, for Pa coming back.

'How can you believe that?' Martha was saying. 'God made us, just like we are now. He made all the creatures, just like they are now. All special and separate. Mum never taught me about any of this! About things changing into other things—'

'Evolving,' I reminded her.

'Well, evolving, changing, whatever—it's not in my biology books!'

'Hang on!' I protested.

But she didn't give me the chance to argue. She dropped her sketch book. Then slammed her hands over her ears. 'I'm not listening! I'm not listening! I'm not listening!' she shrieked at me.

Then she took off into the hills, running like a hare.

I stared after her. Then ran desperately to Ma, flung my arms out wide, 'What did I do wrong? What did I do?'

She looked vaguely at me, 'Don't ask me,' she shrugged.

76

Her mind was on other things. The Whirligig Theatre Company van was bumping up the track to Broom Cottage. 'Hope your dad's got some answers from those Aqua North crooks,' she was saying.

I turned round to watch Martha running away. She hadn't got very far. She kept stumbling, tripping over rocks. It's hard to make any progress with your hands jammed over your ears.

'What did I do?' I appealed hopelessly to Chingwe. 'I only said about people coming from chimps. What's wrong with that?'

Chingwe grunted and scratched his belly. He picked up a shiny blue beetle. He brought it very close to his face and inspected its waving legs. He smacked his lips. Then made them into a funnel . . .

I didn't wait to watch him eat it. I picked Martha's sketch book up and started running after her.

'Wait for me!' I yelled, even though I knew she wasn't listening.

Ten

How did I know? I was thinking as I went after Martha.
How did I know she didn't know about evolution and all
that other stuff?

I could hardly believe it. I'd never met anyone who hadn't
heard of dinosaurs. I couldn't understand why it had upset
her so much, or why she'd run away.

Maybe it was Chingwe, I thought as I scrambled up a dry
ravine. Maybe she doesn't want to be related to him.

I could hardly believe it was that either. I didn't mind
being related to Chingwe. I felt quite proud of it actually.
Chingwe had brains—he had feelings. You only had to look
in his eyes to see that. There was a lot going on inside
Chingwe's little coconut-head.

I had to stop thinking. Climbing took all my
concentration. It was tough going. You could break a leg
here—dead easy. There were wide cracks in the limestone,
as if there'd been an earthquake. And potholes, like dark
wells sunk in the rock. Some were so deep that, if you threw
a stone down them, you couldn't hear it hit bottom.

Martha was up there, on a slope high above me. She was
using both hands to climb. She'd have to listen to me now.

'Martha, I've got your drawings!' I yelled up at her.

She didn't stop. I had a sudden, brilliant idea to grab her
attention: 'Hey, Martha, want to see a dinosaur?'

That stopped her all right.

She came skidding back down the slope in an avalanche
of dust and pebbles. I looked anxiously at her face. She
didn't look mad any more. She was frowning, as if she was
hurt.

'Did you fall over?' I asked her.

She gave a quick, impatient shake of her head. 'You told me these dinosaur things were extinct.'

'Well, they are. But I found one in the caves. He's not alive, of course. He hasn't been alive for, I don't know, a hundred million years or something. I just found his bones.'

'Show me,' was all Martha said. She was rubbing the scar over her eye, as if she could rub it away.

I thought I'd better keep off the topic of being related to Chingwe—I didn't want to upset her again. But I was dead keen to tell her about dinosaurs. I'd been bananas about them once. I still thought they were magic. I felt sorry for her—I thought that anyone who didn't know about dinosaurs had a deprived childhood.

So, I was eager to give her some info on T-Rex and three-horned Triceratops and all the rest of the dinosaur gang. Then I took one look at her grim, unsmiling face. 'Keep your mouth shut, Nemo,' I warned myself. It seemed like even dinosaurs were going to be a touchy subject.

Instead, I looked round to get my bearings. I said, 'You know that place where I came out the cave and gave you your drawing book? Here's your drawings again by the way.' I held the book out and she took it without a word. 'Anyhow, you know that place?'

'We're standing nearly on top of it,' she said. She knew these hills much better than I did. 'Look, it's over here.'

'Oh . . . right,' I said slowly. 'Well, I've got no sense of direction, have I? Anyhow, the dinosaur is down there, in the cave.'

She was already kneeling down, to peer through the hole. She took her knife and in a few quick, urgent slashes, cut away some more tree roots.

'Come on then. I want to see these bones.'

'What if I go first?' I suggested. 'I mean, I've got the torch.'

She moved aside. 'Put that knife away, will you, please?' I asked her, very politely.

It made me nervous. It hadn't before. But then, she'd seemed like a different person before, when she didn't know about evolution.

I thought, Wish I'd never mentioned it! It wasn't the sort of chat-up line you usually use with girls. In fact, you could go out with girls loads of times and never even mention it.

'But *you* had to go and bring it up, didn't you?' I sneered at myself as we picked our way down the limestone staircase. 'You and your big mouth!'

I was having serious second thoughts now. Wondering if it was a good idea to show Martha the dinosaur. What if she got angry again? Or blocked up her ears and ran away?

By now, we were standing on the sandy cave floor. I'd switched off the torch. I was trying to figure out what to do for the best, while in the background, what was left of Hope Spring went drip, drip, drip, down the wall.

Drip, drip, drip.

Martha shuffled impatiently beside me in the darkness. 'So where are these bones?'

Suddenly, I thought, Christ, just do it. I was pig-sick of *thinking*. Pig-sick of trying to work out every angle, watching my mouth all the time. It just wasn't my style. It tied my brain into knots.

The old reckless Nemo, Nemo the showman, came swooping back in like Superman!

Click, I flipped on my torch like a spotlight.

'Ladies and gentlemen!' My showman's voice rang round that cave, as if we had a big, big audience.

'And now, ladies and gentlemen, *perleese* welcome the tiny star of our show . . . '

A circle of white light hit the wall. The raptor sprang out of the dark!

'Comp . . . sog . . . nathus!' I cried. And, boy, did I feel better. I felt like Ma bursting out of her corset.

The echoes of my voice died away, 'Nathus, nathus, nathus.'

'Well, what do you think?' I asked Martha, eagerly. 'He's beautiful, isn't he? He's only little but look at those claws on his toes. He's a killing machine. A predator. Really dangerous. Rip you apart those claws could. He'd spring at you feet-first, then *rippp* . . . '

Silence.

I thought, for a few frantic seconds, You've done it now, Nemo. Bet she's upset again. Or she thinks you're a show-off. She probably thinks, He really fancies himself!

But it wasn't any of those things. Because, when she spoke, it was about hawks, not about me. And she sounded excited. You could practically see her brain fizzing away, making connections. She said, 'Hawks do that. I've watched them, loads of times. They attack feet-first like that, grab with their claws.'

'No, no, no,' I said, shaking my head and grinning. I couldn't help sounding a bit patronizing—she had such a lot to learn. 'You don't understand. These dinosaurs were like big lizards. Giant lizards.'

'Well, this one is a bird,' said Martha. 'Look at its long pointy skull, that's a bird skull.'

'It's got *teeth* in it,' I said, still grinning. How wrong could she be?

'It's still a bird skull,' she insisted. 'Here, shine the light on my drawing book. Just look.'

I knew it was stupid. But she sounded so confident, so sure of herself. So I looked at her sketches of hawk skulls. I shone the torch again on the raptor, then back at the skulls. There was something stirring deep down in my brain—one of the facts I used to know about dinosaurs, trying to push its way to the surface.

'And look at its foot,' said Martha, the words tumbling out of her mouth. 'That's a bird foot—I've drawn one here—see, with four toes. And the shape of the skeleton, see, those arm bones are like wing bones and it's even got a wishbone—look at its breastbone, just look! That's what you pull and make a wish on when you have a turkey at Christmas. Birds have those. *Only* birds.'

'Hmmmmm,' I said.

That fact I used to know—I'd remembered it now. I'd remembered that birds don't come from pterodactyls like you'd think they do. No. They evolved from little raptors like this one. That's what my dinosaur books told me.

'And anyway,' said Martha, decisively. 'It's got feathers.'

'Those are ferns,' I said. But my voice didn't sound so sure any more.

''Course they're not,' said Martha. 'They're its feathers.'

She traced the delicate outline with her fingers, 'See?' And I suddenly knew they were feathers too.

My brain was doing loop-the-loops. I could hardly get the words out: 'Do you know what we've found? Do you know what we've found?' I kept asking, in a dazed voice. 'That's a feathered dinosaur. That's a dino-bird up there! Scientists would kill for that fossil. It's a missing link between dinosaurs and birds. Like Chingwe's probably a missing link, between chimps and us. See, it's evolution, that's the way it works. Things changing, slowly changing all the time. I told you! I told you it wasn't rubbish, didn't I?'

Martha was still tracing the feathers. She seemed to be in a dream.

I tried again. 'Look, I know it's a shock and everything. I mean, if I wanted to be a biologist, like you do, and there was all this stuff no one had told *me*, well I'd be mad too.'

I thought I'd better shut up before my big mouth got me into trouble.

'I'm not mad,' said Martha. 'I guessed already.'

82

'What?' I said, totally confused. 'I thought you didn't know about any of this?'

'Well, I didn't actually know. I mean, not for certain. I guessed though. I guessed there was more than what Mum and Dad had taught me—when I found this stone-thing.'

She pulled the piece of rock from her jeans pocket—the one she'd tried to show me before but I hadn't had time to really look at.

I shone the torch on it.

'It's some kind of fossil,' I said.

It was some kind of very primitive creature—it looked like a giant woodlouse. 'Bet that's old,' I told her. 'Older than dinosaurs,' I added vaguely trying to remember what I knew about fossils. I wasn't red-hot on the subject of fossils—not like I was on dinosaurs. 'I *think* those ones are called trilobites. The ones that—'

'I know,' said Martha. 'The ones that crawled out of the swamp and became land creatures—'

'You got it.'

'No, I haven't,' she said, miserably. 'All I got is questions. Loads and loads of questions. I've got to re-think *everything* now!'

Her voice sounded strange, sort of choked. She bit her lip, it was trembling. I swished the torch beam away from her face to give her some privacy. She's crying, I thought desperately. What have I done now?

But she didn't mention me when she spoke.

'They lied to me—about biology.'

'Who lied?'

'Mum and Dad.'

'Naa,' I said, trying to comfort her. 'Your mum and dad wouldn't lie. They're really nice people, aren't they? Maybe they don't know about evolution and dinosaurs either.'

Martha sniffed, stopped crying, rubbed at her eyes with her fists. 'Well, they've never even mentioned dinosaurs.'

I shrugged. 'That must be it then. They don't know about them.'

Even as I was saying this, I thought it sounded really far-fetched. I mean, you'd have to have come from Mars not to know about dinosaurs.

'I'll tell them!' said Martha, full of excitement, as if she'd discovered a whole new world. 'They'll think it's brilliant! I'll show them this dinosaur. I'll tell them about—'

'Maaaartha.' From above our heads came a soft, menacing whisper. There it was again, 'Maaaartha.'

I jumped a mile. I felt the hairs lifting up on the back of my neck. 'What the hell was that?'

Martha looked up. 'It's only Dad. What's he doing here? Hi, Dad.'

She slid the trilobite quickly back in her pocket. I whisked the torch away from the feathered dinosaur. I didn't want Mr le Duke to know about it. I didn't know why, exactly. It was just a gut reaction.

My torch beam crossed another beam. It came from the light on Mr le Duke's hard yellow hat. He was halfway up the rock wall, staring down at us. He looked like some mighty cave-dwelling giant, the Lord of Cave World. He filled the slash in the rock, where Hope Spring used to come hammering down.

I wondered how long he'd been up there; what he'd seen and heard.

His whispering voice had scared me half to death. But he was smiling now. His blue eyes were fixed directly on me, as if I was the only one in the cave. They didn't acknowledge Martha at all.

'Hi there, son!' he called down. He sounded very cheerful, as if he was pleased to see me. That made me feel proud.

I smiled back at him, 'Hi, Mr le Duke.'

All my uneasy feelings about him faded away. I was impressed all over again. Hypnotized by those clear blue eyes. I was 100 per cent certain Mr le Duke would never tell a lie. At that moment, I would have trusted him with my life.

'Come up here, son,' called Mr le Duke. 'This tunnel is another way out. There's something at the end of it I'd like you to see.'

'I can't get up there,' I told him.

'Don't be a doubter, son! Yes, you can.'

And like a stairway to heaven, a rope ladder unfurled and cascaded down the cave wall.

'Just shin up that, son. Bet you can climb like a monkey.'

I thought, Well, I can climb better than Chingwe anyway. But that wasn't saying much.

'Come on, son,' he coaxed me, his voice still friendly. 'I'm waiting.'

You don't keep Mr le Duke waiting. I only hesitated for a second. Then I rushed to obey him.

Martha grabbed my arm. 'Can I borrow your torch a minute?'

She called to her dad, 'I'm coming up right away, Dad. I've just got to do a quick sketch.'

I scrambled up the ladder. I was buzzing with curiosity, wondering what Mr le Duke wanted me to see. It made me feel warm inside, as if he'd singled me out for some special privilege.

I followed him through the tunnel, slithering on greasy mud, splashing through puddles. The tunnel narrowed suddenly. I clashed my head off the roof. 'Ouch!'

I wondered how Mr le Duke was squeezing his big body through. He was a little way ahead of me. I could see the star-pattern on the soles of his boots.

The light on his hard hat made a soft glow in the darkness.

Then suddenly his boots disappeared. There was a hard, glaring light. It flooded into the tunnel, nearly blinding me.

'Careful now, son,' said Mr le Duke. 'I'll help you down.'

I felt myself gently swung through the air by strong arms. I was set down on a rocky floor. I opened my eyes, stared about me, half-dazzled.

I thought I was outside in the sunshine. Then I realized I wasn't. I was still underground, in another cave, lit by brilliant electric lights.

'Welcome to our bunker,' said Mr le Duke. 'We'll all be safe here, when Armageddon comes.'

Eleven

'Wow!' I said, gazing around. I was really amazed. The caves I'd been in so far had been dark places. Cluttered with stalagmites, stalactites, limestone blocks, fossils. They felt ancient and mysterious.

But this one was lit up like an airport runway. It had been cleared of rubble and tree roots. It was packed with stores. Tin foil cartons, neatly stacked, crates, gas masks, spades, engine parts, a first aid box. It looked like some sort of underground HQ.

All sorts of questions were bouncing around in my brain. I didn't know which one to ask first.

'What's in them?' I pointed to the cartons.

Mr le Duke seemed pleased by my enthusiasm.

'They're food rations,' he said. 'Meals Ready-to-Eat. Used by the military in training situations—or combat.'

'Combat?' I said, all excited. 'You a soldier, Mr le Duke?' I wouldn't have been a bit surprised.

'No, no, son,' smiled Mr le Duke, shaking his head. 'I'm just an ordinary family man. I don't like violence. I just need to protect my family, that's all.'

I thought about Martha and Mrs le Duke in her flowery frock, with the little girls crowding round her.

'Nobody's going to hurt them, are they?' I asked Mr le Duke, urgently. 'You tell me who's going to hurt them and I'll kill them. I will! I'll—'

I stopped. I could hear my mouth flapping, hear myself going way, way over the top. I could hear my dad saying, 'Calm down, Nemo.'

But Mr le Duke didn't tell me to calm down. He seemed to approve. His eyes glittered encouragement.

He patted me on the shoulder. 'You're a good boy, son,' he said. 'That's the right spirit. We'll need a fighting spirit like yours when the crisis comes.'

I couldn't help glowing with pride when Mr le Duke praised me. But at the same time, I was getting very confused.

'What crisis?' I asked him. 'Is something awful going to happen?'

'Well, I'll tell you, son,' said Mr le Duke.

He looked serious. He sat down on a crate as if he was going to tell me a story.

'Once upon a time,' he began, 'the sinners of this world were wiped out in the Great Flood. Like it says in the Bible, only Noah and his family were saved because they were righteous people. That time is coming again. Armageddon is coming when all the sinners will be called to account. And only the righteous will survive.'

'You mean,' I said struggling to understand, 'that there's going to be another Great Flood?'

'Precisely, son,' said Mr le Duke. 'Either a flood, or this time it might be plague or chemical warfare or drought. We have to be prepared for anything. We may have to defend ourselves.'

My mouth opened, then closed. I couldn't think of the right words to say. I looked around for Martha to help me. Then I remembered that she was still in the other cave, sketching the dino-bird.

Mr le Duke was watching me very closely. I had to say something. 'Oh, right,' I said, nodding my head.

I couldn't stand his intense blue gaze. It seemed to be burning me up. My eyes slid away from his. They flickered nervously about the cave. There was a small side chamber— I hadn't noticed it before. It had a heavy grille over the entrance. Inside was a strange steel box. Like a wardrobe, only longer and thinner.

'What's in there?' I asked Mr le Duke, just to give myself time to think.

When he answered his voice was perfectly calm, as if he was discussing the weather. 'Weapons,' he said. 'I told you, we may have to defend ourselves.'

'You're kidding me!' I was really interested. 'What weapons?'

'Two AK-47 assault rifles,' said Mr le Duke, ticking off on his fingers, 'two 45-millimetre Smith and Wessons, a high-powered hunting rifle, two crossbows, and some combat knives.'

I could hear the pride in his voice as he went through the list.

'Can I see them?' I asked him. I suddenly thought of Martha's combat knife. I knew now where she'd got it.

'I don't think so, son,' said Mr le Duke kindly. 'Maybe one day. Maybe one day I'll even teach you how to use them.'

I liked the idea of that—it gave me a shiver of excitement. I'd have to be careful not to tell Ma, though. She hated guns. I could already hear her yelling at me, 'Guns! No son of mine is having anything to do with guns! They ought to ban the whole lot of them! Melt them all down in a big furnace!'

'Isn't it against the law,' I said, without thinking, 'to have weapons like that?'

'Against whose laws?' asked Mr le Duke. 'I don't acknowledge any laws but God's.'

'Oh . . . right,' I said again, very slowly and carefully.

I was out of my depth here. There was a big struggle going on in my mind. I knew what Ma would say. She would say Mr le Duke was nuts. But it was hard to see that when you were listening to him. Sitting there on the crate, he looked really convincing. He looked tough, powerful, as if he could handle those weapons, as if he could handle anything. His voice was quiet and reasonable. And his blue eyes blazed with belief. You just couldn't help giving him respect.

I frowned. 'So this Armageddon thing, do you know when it's going to happen?'

'Of course I do,' said Mr le Duke. 'That's why I'm making preparations. It will happen at the millennium. In the year 2000.'

And he sounded so absolutely certain about this, like he sounded certain about everything, that I didn't even dream of contradicting him or saying, 'How do you know?'

'But,' said Mr le Duke, smiling, 'there's no need to despair. There will always be room for the righteous in our bunker. Especially for righteous neighbours. Are you righteous, son? Is your family righteous?'

That really threw me. No one had ever asked me questions like that before. I thought, wildly, Well, I don't know, do I?

But I knew one thing—Mr le Duke expected a clear yes or no answer. I opened my mouth. I had no idea what was going to come out, 'Er . . . er . . . '

Martha saved me. She came shooting out of the tunnel. She stopped for a moment, dazzled by the bright lights, like I'd been. She stared round, as if this place was new to her too.

Then she burst out, 'Dad! Do you want to see a dinosaur?'

Mr le Duke's eyes switched from me to her.

He didn't seem surprised at such a weird question. And it flashed through my mind that he already knew all about the feathered dinosaur. That he'd been up in the tunnel mouth for a long time, listening to everything me and Martha had been saying. It would have been easy to hear us. We hadn't been whispering. Our voices had been really loud, excited.

Martha was still excited. Her sketch book was open in her hand, ready to show him. 'Dad, there's millions of years to find out about. All about evolution—'

90

Mr le Duke's sudden, harsh laugh interrupted her. It shocked me because I'd never heard him laugh that way before. I mean, he had perfect manners. But now he was shaking his head—he seemed really amused. His blue eyes danced with laughter. 'I know,' he said. 'People descended from apes. It's a good joke, isn't it?'

'You already knew about it?' asked Martha. She sounded bewildered and shocked. 'Why didn't you tell me?'

Mr le Duke's voice was soothing now. As if he was talking to a little kid who'd got hold of some foolish notions.

'The story of how life began is in the Bible, Martha,' he told her. 'And that story is all you need to know.'

'But all those biology books you gave me!' said Martha. 'Why didn't they say about it? I studied them and studied them. But I didn't see evolution written one single time!'

'Do you think your mother and I would let you read books that put wrong ideas into your head?' said Mr le Duke, kindly. 'We sent away specially for those books. Because they don't teach children stupid ideas.'

'But I wanted to *know*!' Martha cried out in an agonized voice. 'Even if you think it's stupid! I still want to know! Other kids know. Why can't I know? Then I can make up my mind for myself.'

Then I made a terrible mistake. You know my big mouth? Well, I couldn't keep quiet any longer. I just opened my mouth up and let it flap.

'Evolution isn't stupid!' I said. 'People coming from apes isn't stupid. You don't really think it's stupid, do you, Martha? What about the dinosaur bird? Show your dad your drawing.'

Martha seemed a bit reluctant. She hesitated. Then she pushed the sketch book at Mr le Duke.

It was a brilliant drawing. Dino-bird was there on the page. Just like he looked on the cave wall—his rib cage, his long, thin tail, his snarling skull. And every delicate feather drawn in. He was just perfect.

I said to her, 'I wish I could draw like that.' I was really impressed. Then I looked up at Mr le Duke. 'See what it is?' I told him eagerly. 'It's a dinosaur, evolving into a bird.'

Mr le Duke hardly glanced at the drawing.

'All I see,' he said scornfully, 'is some kind of fantasy creature. A silly child getting carried away by her own imagination.'

He tossed the drawing aside, as if it was just *rubbish*!

I couldn't believe it. I was practically jumping out of my skin with frustration. 'But it's not out of Martha's head! It's in the next cave. You saw it, didn't you?'

'I saw *nothing*.'

He seemed absolutely, 100 per cent sure. I daren't argue with him, say, 'Yes you did!' so I said, 'But you could go and see it now. Honest, Mr le Duke, it really exists, it's there on the wall. You can touch it—you can touch its bones!'

Mr le Duke's lip curled as if I'd said something gross. He shot me a look. That look advised me, *'Son, this subject is at an end.'*

But I've always been useless at taking advice. And, anyway, I was too fired up to stop now. 'What about Chingwe then?' I appealed to Mr le Duke. 'He's not just bones. He's living, breathing proof! Dr Dekler was nearly certain about it. He just wanted to do some experiments to prove it but 'course I said no. *"No way,"* I said and then Ma said—'

Afterwards, I wished I'd shut up. I wished I'd taken notice of the warning lights flashing in Martha's eyes. But I didn't. I was too desperate to make Mr le Duke understand. I really thought I could do it. I really believed that no one could get to know Chingwe, could look into his eyes, and still say that humans coming from apes was just a joke.

'Who's Chingwe, son?' Mr le Duke asked, in his soft-spoken voice. He sounded very polite again now, almost gentle.

But Martha's eyes were still sending me frantic danger signals. *'Don't tell him any more. Don't.'*

It was too late. I couldn't stop myself boasting about Chingwe.

'Chingwe's my humanzee,' I told Mr le Duke, proudly. 'I rescued him. He's really special, He's sort of half human, half chimp.'

'And this thing is *alive*?' frowned Mr le Duke. It was the first time I'd seen him look rattled.

''Course he's alive. He lives at our house. Martha's seen him, haven't you Martha?'

'Is this true, daughter?' said Mr le Duke, turning towards Martha.

Martha hesitated. But she couldn't resist that stare. It seemed to X-ray your brain. Search out lies before you even told them. She nodded, then lowered her head.

'This thing sounds like an abomination. Not something created by God,' said Mr le Duke, very quietly.

'Hey, wait a second!' I protested.

My respect for Mr le Duke was still strong. But my loyalty to Chingwe was stronger. I mean, Chingwe really meant a lot to me. And nobody, not even Mr le Duke, had the right to insult him like that.

'You shouldn't call Chingwe a thing!' I told Mr le Duke, indignantly. 'He's . . . well . . . he's Chingwe, isn't he? And anyhow Dr Dekler says he's probably pretty big news. Like an evolutionary bombshell, that's what he said! Like, the living ultimate proof that we're all descended from apes.'

'Who knows about this bombshell,' asked Mr le Duke, staring at me. 'Who knows where he is? Who *exactly*?'

That deep-blue gaze made me flinch. I thought at the time it was a weird question. But I couldn't think of any instant reason not to answer it. So I just went babbling on.

93

'Well, Dr Dekler, from the Primate Rehabilitation Centre, he knows where we live. And Martha knows and my ma and pa, of course—and now you know. I think that's all. We've kept a bit quiet about him. Because there'd be big publicity if people found out. Dr Dekler said so. He wanted to keep Chingwe, he was really desperate. He said, ''I'll make this chimp famous. I'll tell the world about him.'' But I wouldn't let them keep him, no way! I wouldn't let them open up Chingwe's brain—'

Suddenly, Mr le Duke seemed to lose interest in Chingwe—and in me.

He got off the crate. Began to sort through his stockpile of army meals.

'I'm sorry to chase you off like this, son. Really sorry. But I've got important work to do.' He sounded apologetic.

Martha began to move over towards me, as if she wanted to leave with me.

But Mr le Duke flashed her one, single look. She stopped dead in her tracks. 'And Martha has some lessons to learn,' he said, not even looking at her now.

'There's the way out, son,' said Mr le Duke, pointing to a wooden stairway that led out of the cave. 'You can get to the surface that way.'

I felt confused. Why did he suddenly want to get rid of me? Just when we seemed to be getting on so well? Just when he'd even offered to teach me to shoot?

'I'll . . . I'll see you again soon then,' I said, feebly.

'That's right, son,' said Mr le Duke, turning his back on me, dismissing me. 'See you soon.'

'See you, Martha,' I said.

Martha said nothing. Just lifted her head. But there was a look on her face—as if she was pleading with me to do something.

What? What do you want me to do? I thought. I raised my eyebrows in a big question mark, trying to make her tell me.

But she wouldn't speak, or give me any sign.

I trudged up the long, wooden stairway that Mr le Duke had built for easy access to his underground bunker. The silence below me was embarrassing. It felt like both of them were watching me, every step of the way.

Halfway up I turned round. I wanted to say something that would get Mr le Duke back on my side, make him approve of me again.

'I'll tell Ma and Pa what you said about there being room in your bunker for good neighbours,' I called back down to him.

Mr le Duke's eyes drilled into mine. There was no warmth in them any more, even though his voice was still soft and very polite. 'I think, son,' he told me, 'that I was too hasty. I think I might have to review that invitation.'

Twelve

My head was spinning as I climbed slowly out of the bunker. What did he mean, 'I might have to review that invitation'?

And what was all that stuff about Armageddon anyway? And what was he doing with his own private armoury?

Down in the cave, looking into Mr le Duke's hypnotic blue eyes, it had all seemed perfectly reasonable. The kind of precautions any family man might take as the Millennium drew near.

I'd even started thinking, Why isn't my pa building a bunker, getting hold of some guns?

But the higher I climbed, the closer I got to the outside world, the crazier it all seemed.

I kept thinking about Martha. I daren't turn round to look back at her. But I could guess what was going on in her head. That's because I knew what it was like to get worked up about something, to care about it. I mean really care *a lot*. Like I did about acting Spike's death scene. Like she did about that drawing. And then have somebody mock your real, true feelings, trample all over them like they were just *trash*. It felt like the rawest, sharpest pain. It made you flinch every time you remembered it. And it took a long, long time to get over it.

I bet I knew what she was doing though. I bet she was rubbing that scar. She did it whenever she got worried about something. I've got habits like that too. Only with me, it's twisting my ear-ring.

I was surprised at Mr le Duke. Surprised he could be so cruel. Surprised that he'd kept Martha in the dark about dinosaurs and fossils and evolution and stuff—things every kid's got a right to know about.

I shook my head, bewildered. Mr le Duke had seemed like one of the good guys. But now he was a big puzzle. I didn't know what to think about him any more. I was even a little bit scared of him.

It seemed like a long climb. But I'd reached the top of the wooden stairway. There was a heavy metal door fitted into the rock. I pushed it open.

The sun hit me, *wham*, like a hammer. Where was I?

There were smooth pebbles under my feet. I was in a gully. Water must once have flowed through here. Now it was dust-dry. Not even a trickle between the stones. There were banks on both sides of me. I couldn't see over them— they were too steep to climb.

So I just followed the river bed.

It took a sharp left turn. Then I couldn't go any further. Blocking my way was a massive pile of earth and rocks. A tree had been felled into the gully. Then limestone boulders and tons of earth had been tipped in to fill it completely.

What's that doing here? I thought, my heart beating faster. My brain was full of awful suspicions, twittering away like a caveful of bats.

It was easy to climb. I scrambled up and looked over the top.

'It's a dam,' I whispered.

Behind the dam, water sparkled in the sun. More water than I'd seen for a long, long time.

Someone had diverted the river. They'd dammed it and dug out a channel to a reservoir, big as a swimming pool. And from there, pipes in trenches took the water away. It was a really neat job. Some of it overflowed into small waterfalls that went down in steps to irrigate the land.

The le Dukes had their own, private, man-made water system. It's what I'd seen, glittering behind their house.

97

Now I was up high, on top of the dam, I could see where I was. I was *inside* the le Dukes' compound. The house and outbuildings were on my right. The electric fence closed the whole place in, like a prison. There was no one around. It was hot and quiet and still. Just a few bees went, 'Buzzzz' in the gorse. There was so much water and I couldn't even raise a spit. I could hardly swallow. My throat felt dry and tight.

I walked over springy grass to the reservoir. The hills around the le Duke compound were dust-dry, bleached white, crumbling. The le Duke's kingdom was a little green oasis in the middle of a desert.

Their water was pure and clear.

I dipped my sweaty face into their water and gulped some of it down. I came up spluttering, drops flying off my hair.

Their water tasted of flowers.

'It's Hope Spring.'

I thought it was, from the moment I saw the dam. I thought it might be our water.

For the first time I understood the geography of Hope Spring. I could picture it mapped out in my head. How it flowed in a river above ground. Then right where the steel door was now, plunged into the cave. Through Mr le Duke's Armageddon bunker. Then through the Compsognathus chamber. Then through a maze of cracks and tunnels. And, on its way, bubbled up into our back yard at Broom Cottage. At least, it *had* bubbled up, until Mr le Duke decided to dam it for his own personal use.

He needn't have taken it all, I was thinking. He could have left some for us.

I could hardly believe he'd do such a selfish thing. There was more water here than one family could ever need— much, much more.

I was outraged at the le Dukes. They're the crooks! I thought. It wasn't the water company at all!

Then I was ashamed of myself.

'Just calm down,' I told myself. 'Don't go bananas. They wouldn't do it *deliberately*. They don't realize what they've done, that's all. They don't know it's our water too. All you need to do is tell them,' I reassured myself. 'Then they'll undam Hope Spring. And we can all share it. The le Dukes and the Whirligig Theatre Company, sharing their water, like good neighbours should.'

Right on cue, a voice behind me said, 'Nemo, you look troubled, is there anything I can help you with?' It sounded really concerned.

I whipped round. It was Mrs le Duke. I was glad it was her, not him. I was sure she'd be easier to talk to. That she'd understand about Hope Spring.

'Well,' I said apologetically, 'there's a bit of a problem.' I swept my arm over the dazzling water. 'You've cut off our water supply. It used to come underground, to our house through the caves. But you've dammed it up, see. I mean, I know you didn't know what you were doing, or you wouldn't have done it. But can we have our water back, please?'

I was already thinking of their faces, Ma and Pa and Chingwe, when the fresh water came bubbling through again. I could imagine Chingwe hooting, 'Hoo, hoo, hoo,' as the dry pit filled up. It'd probably scare him. Chimps don't like water—Dr Dekler said that.

Mrs le Duke looked really apologetic too. I thought, I knew she'd understand.

She said, in her gentle voice, 'That's impossible, I'm afraid. We're using the caves for storage now. We couldn't let water through there again. You can see that, Nemo, can't you?'

I couldn't believe she was turning me down; I thought my ears were playing tricks on me. Then I thought, You haven't explained it properly! She hasn't understood how important it is.

So I tried to make her see. 'We've got to have water,' I pleaded with her. 'We've got to have Hope Spring. It's like really, desperately important to us. We can't live here without it. We'll have to leave our home! Then what will we do?'

She listened, her head bent to one side with that same kind, concerned look on her face. I thought, She understands, at last.

But then she shook her head. 'We have to prepare,' she said. 'Water is precious now. When Armageddon comes, people will be fighting for every drop there is.'

I just stared at her. She looked calmly back at me.

And at last *I* understood. It was like an explosion of light in my brain. They're stockpiling water, I thought, horrified. Like they're stockpiling food and fuel and guns.

I got really worked up then. 'But you don't need all this! What about us? We're neighbours, aren't we? Don't we matter?'

'The righteous must survive,' said Mrs le Duke. 'God wills it. They must take whatever they need to survive.'

She'd made it perfectly clear. But part of me still couldn't accept it. 'Are you saying you're not going to give us our water back? No way?'

'God wills it,' said Mrs le Duke.

'No, he doesn't!' I yelled at her. 'He wants you to share it.'

There wasn't the smallest flicker of doubt or uneasiness in her eyes. It was spooky—she still had that same calm smile. She knew our lives would be ruined. She understood that. But that wasn't going to change her mind.

Then I knew it was hopeless.

And for the first time, I started to feel *really* afraid of the le Dukes.

I turned away. She didn't move. She just stood there, seeing me off their property, like I was an enemy or something.

'You're getting paranoid again, Nemo,' I told myself. 'Just calm down.'

But I couldn't help hurrying to get to the other side of the fence.

The gates were closed. I didn't dare open them. I thought, What if the electricity's switched on?

Then I thought, Don't be stupid. It was just another preparation. They wouldn't need the electric fence until Armageddon—to keep out all the thirst-crazed, starving unrighteous prowling around outside.

I stretched out my hand. Then I remembered Boss. The way he bounced off the fence in a shower of blue sparks. The way he howled.

Then someone came up behind me, reached past me and pushed the gate open. It was Martha.

'Hi!' I said, giving her a big smile. I was really pleased to see her.

She glanced back, over her shoulder, as if someone was watching from the house, checking up on us.

When she spoke, her voice sounded distant and strange.

'My dad says I can't see you any more,' she said.

'Tell him to go to hell!' I told her. 'Tell him you see who you like!'

'You don't understand. No one talks to my dad like that.'

A dreadful thought came boiling into my brain. 'Does he hit you or anything? What about that scar?' I pointed to the pink moon on her forehead. 'Did he do that? I'll kill him if he did. Is he cruel to you? I'll kill him!'

She seemed really shocked. She frowned and rubbed at the scar. Then realized she was doing it and snatched her hand away. 'No, no, 'course he didn't do this. How could you say that? I did it years and years ago when I fell over. You don't understand—Dad's never laid a finger on any of us. He loves us. He only wants to protect us.'

'That's all right, then,' I muttered, feeling a bit of a prat.

101

She looked back at the windows of the house. Then she said, 'Take these for me.' It was her sketch book, open at the drawing of the feathered dinosaur, and the trilobite fossil she'd found. She slipped them to me, secretly, as if they were dangerous things.

'Keep them safe,' she said, 'and say hello to Chingwe for me. It was great meeting him. I wouldn't be surprised, you know—'

'Surprised about what?'

'I wouldn't be surprised if Chingwe really was a humanzee . . . ' Then she said, 'I've got to go now.'

'Stay a bit longer.' I had this terrible feeling that if I let her go now I wasn't going to see her again. And I liked her, you know. I was really starting to like her.

'I can't stay,' she said.

For once, I couldn't find any words. Me, Nemo, with nothing to say!

I felt helpless.

I just stood and watched while she walked back to her house and went inside. Somebody shut the door behind her.

Thirteen

I stumbled back to Broom Cottage carrying Martha's drawings and her trilobite.

I'd lost all track of time. I checked my watch—it was way past lunch time. No wonder my belly was rumbling. I felt dead tired too—I hadn't got much sleep last night in the van.

I just couldn't cope with what had happened that morning. A whole crowd of questions tormented me. But the main thing I kept asking myself was: 'How could they? How could they?'

I just couldn't understand it. The le Dukes had seemed like such nice people. Nice, reliable, friendly, people; the kind of folk you could trust. So how could they keep all that water for themselves? When they knew that someone else desperately needed some?

How could they stop Martha from seeing me?

It really upset me, even more than the water. It was personal. I thought, What am I supposed to have done that's so terrible? I'd never made one single move—not even asked her to go out with me or anything.

It's not as if I didn't *think* about asking her out—because I did. But things had been moving so fast there just hadn't been the time. And now it looked like I'd lost my chance.

I thought, Maybe I showed off too much or something. Whatever I'd done, I'd made a real mess of things.

I kicked at a pebble to let off some steam. It zinged like a bullet off a rock. It didn't make me feel any better. In a frenzy of kicking I booted every pebble I saw: *Zing, zing, zing, zing.* A little voice warned me, 'You're going bananas,

Nemo, calm down.' But I thought, so what! Ma would go more than bananas when she found out about Hope Spring. She'd go ballistic.

I could just imagine her: 'What's this guy's name that stole our water? Mr le Duke? Wait until I get my hands on him. I'll kill him! I'll make dogmeat of him. I'll make him wish he'd never been born!'

'Course, Ma would never hurt a fly really. She rescues spiders out of the bath. She's a pacifist. She just talks like that because, well, she's a bit over-dramatic.

Then another thought hit me, a really frightening thought. It made me stop dead. 'You can't tell her,' I decided, out loud.

I thought about that visionary look in Mr le Duke's blue eyes. Mr le Duke wasn't playing games. He was on a deadly serious mission, preparing for Armageddon. Anyone who crossed him, anyone who got in his way . . .

'Naa, don't get carried away,' I tried to reassure myself. 'He wouldn't hurt Ma.'

But, all the same, I didn't trust him any more.

I decided to tell Pa first, about the water. You could trust Pa to keep cool, to keep his head. He wouldn't go rushing off to threaten a man with a steel case full of guns.

I was already shouting, 'Pa!' when I ran into Broom Cottage.

But what I saw there drove the stolen water clean out of my head.

'Chingwe's ill,' Pa told me.

They were in the kitchen. Chingwe was curled up on the floor and Pa was crouching beside him. There were apples, pink grapefruit, and onions scattered around—all of Chingwe's favourite food.

'He won't eat anything,' said Pa, 'not even grapefruit.'

I dropped to my knees beside Chingwe. 'What's he like this for?' I said angrily. I was mad at Pa—but madder at myself for leaving Chingwe for so long. 'What's wrong with him? He was all right this morning. What have you done to him?'

'Don't be a pain, Nemo,' sighed Pa. 'Losing your temper won't help him, will it? We haven't done anything to him. He's sick. It happened really quickly.'

Wearily, Chingwe lifted his wrinkled hand as if to show he knew I was there. He tried to look up. But he was too weak to lift his head. He closed his eyes.

'What's wrong with him, Pa?' I begged. I was really panicking.

I picked up the shaggy hair on Chingwe's back, trying to groom him, but he was too sick to notice.

'I think he's got a cold,' said Pa. 'Just listen.'

I calmed down enough to listen. I could hear Chingwe's snuffling breath.

'His nose is blocked up,' said Pa. 'And he sneezed just now.'

Relief washed over me. 'Well, a cold's not serious, is it? People get colds all the time. I get loads of colds.'

'No you don't,' said Pa. 'And anyway, Chingwe's a chimp, remember. Colds can be very serious in chimps. They can even kill them.'

'Don't talk like that!' I said, frantically, trying to shut him up. I felt like slamming my hands over my ears, like Martha did when I talked about evolution. 'Don't talk like that. Chingwe might hear you!'

'He's gone to sleep,' said Pa. 'He can't hear anything.'

Pa took a deep breath, as if he was psyching himself up to say something I wouldn't like. 'Look, Nemo,' he said, 'you've got to understand. Chingwe's already a very old chimp. Dr Dekler told us that. He said he didn't expect him to last much longer—and that's even without him getting a cold.'

'That creep!' I raged at Pa. 'Don't talk to me about Dr

Dekler! He'd do anything to get his hands on Chingwe. Even on his dead body! So he can do experiments on him, slice up his brain, count his chromosomes and stuff. Don't take any notice of what that creep says! I'll kill him if he comes near Chingwe. I'll—'

'Shhh,' said Pa. 'You'll wake Chingwe up.'

'Oh, sorry.' I stopped raving straight away. Chingwe twitched and moaned. But he didn't wake up.

'We're going to have to call in a vet,' said Pa.

I got frantic all over again. 'No, Pa, he might take Chingwe away from us. Soon as he sees Chingwe's different from other chimps, that he might be a humanzee, he'll take him away. We'll never see him again.'

'All right, then,' Pa agreed. 'But if he gets any worse we *have* to call the vet. Right?'

'Right.' I nodded miserably.

Pa said, 'What's that you're kneeling on?'

'What?' I looked down. I was kneeling on Martha's sketch of the feathered dinosaur. The trilobite was in my jeans' pocket.

If things had been different I would have shown Pa the picture. I would have said, 'We found this brilliant fossil, Pa, and Martha drew it.'

But I was too sick with worry about Chingwe. So I just muttered, 'Oh that, it's nothing.' And I shoved the book out of sight under the kitchen table. 'Pa,' I said, desperately, 'he's going to be all right, isn't he? He's had such a crappy life, shut up in freak shows. And now he's poorly . . . '

It was a weird thing—I hadn't shut Chingwe up in freak shows, I hadn't been cruel to him. But I still felt guilty at the way he'd been treated by humans. I still felt responsible and ashamed, even though I hadn't done it. I wanted to make it up to him somehow.

I could feel my fists clenching tight, because it was such a powerful longing. 'I want him to be happy,' I told Pa. 'Like he would have been if he was in the forests in Africa. When he was free—before the humans caught him and put him in a cage.'

'I know, son, I know,' said Pa, in a solemn voice. 'But look, he probably wouldn't have been happy in the forest either. Remember at the Rehabilitation Centre? How the other apes tried to kill him?'

'Poor humanzee,' I said, smacking my fist in my eye to rub the tears away. 'He doesn't belong with people or chimps. He doesn't belong anywhere, does he, Pa? My poor humanzee.'

Fourteen

All afternoon I kept thinking, I have to tell Pa who's stolen Hope Spring. I have to tell him about Mr le Duke.

I kept puzzling over how to explain Mr and Mrs le Duke to Pa. I didn't know where to begin.

'Look, Pa, there's this guy who thinks Armageddon is coming in the year 2000. So he's made a cave into an underground bunker and he's got all this food down there. And lots of weapons in case the unrighteous attack. And, by the way, he's stolen our water . . . '

Pa would probably say, 'Nemo, have you been at my home-brew beer again?'

As it happened though, I never got the chance to tell Pa. I couldn't catch him on his own. Ma was with us all the time, watching over Chingwe. Like me, she wouldn't leave him. She was worried sick about him.

'He's like family,' she said. 'He's part of the Whirligig Theatre Company.'

I kept telling myself that the water could wait a while. Chingwe was more important than water. We had emergency supplies, stacked round the house in every kind of container. Pa had driven miles to collect it.

So evening came and I still hadn't said anything about the le Dukes. Martha had been on my mind a lot though. I couldn't stop thinking about her. Wondering how I could see her again. Wondering if they'd ever let her out of that compound.

'Martha said to say hello,' I told Chingwe. 'I like her. I mean, she's a good kid. But I don't know if I'll ever get to see her again . . . '

Chingwe's face was as grey as a ghost. His distress call, 'Hoo, hoo, hoo,' was really feeble, like a fluttering baby bird.

'I'm going to call that vet,' said Pa suddenly, leaping up out of his chair.

'No, Pa, he'll take him away!'

'Use your head, Nemo, look at the state of him. I should have called the vet long ago!'

He went over to the phone, started looking numbers up in the Yellow Pages.

I don't know if it was Pa raising his voice—because he hardly ever does—but something made Chingwe sit up. I stared at him, amazed. He reached out for a grapefruit! He didn't have the strength to turn it inside out, so he just clutched it in his hands and mumbled at it with rubbery lips.

'Look, he's better!' I cried out to Pa. 'He wants something to eat!'

I picked up another grapefruit, slashed it in half with a kitchen knife.

'Here, Chingwe, have this one. It's a pink one—they're your favourite.'

Chingwe took the half grapefruit, made his lips into a funnel and began to suck the juice through it.

'He does look a lot better,' said Ma. 'Maybe it was just one of those twenty-four hour bugs.'

Pa put the phone directory down. 'Well, I'm not too sure about that—' he started to say.

'But you can see he's getting better!' I said angrily, daring Pa to contradict me.

'Hey, Chingwe,' I said, looking into Chingwe's intelligent brown eyes. 'You're going to be all right now, aren't you? That Dr Dekler, he didn't know what he was talking about.'

Much later, when it was dark, I took Chingwe out to look at the stars. It was a really warm night. He was still a bit wobbly but he did seem loads better. He seemed like his old self again.

Ma and Pa stayed in the house mending some props. Pa was painting the flea circus ring brilliant white. He said, 'Nemo, I've sent for some new fleas. We've got a show to do in a few days' time.'

Outside there was a massive silver moon—you could see the seas and craters on it. There were no clouds in the sky; it was almost as bright as day. The hills all around Broom Cottage were mysterious and blue in the moonlight.

We sat down by the dry pit of Hope Spring. Seeing it made me feel uneasy, especially now Chingwe was much better. But I thought, I'll tell Pa about it tomorrow. Today I was just too worn out with worrying about Chingwe.

I thought, I'm an emotional wreck! I couldn't face any more aggravation tonight. I couldn't face all the talking it would take, to bring Pa up to speed on the le Duke situation. I needed some peace and quiet. I needed a good night's sleep.

'Soon as I get up,' I promised myself, 'before I do anything else, I'll tell him.'

I knew I should tell him right now, that I was making feeble excuses. But the fact is, I was scared of telling him. Pa against Mr le Duke. That would be no contest. No matter how hard I tried to explain, Pa would have no idea of what Mr le Duke was like—of the powerful, unstoppable force we were up against.

I know Pa, I thought, sighing. He'll think all we need to do is stay *calm*, to go over there and have a cup of tea and talk it out like *reasonable* people.

Chingwe gave a little cough, 'Uff, uff!' I turned to him in alarm.

But he seemed OK—just a tickle in his throat. He was lying on his back gazing into the night sky, looking at all the stars and planets and comets millions of miles out in space. His eyes looked faraway and sparkly, as if they reflected the stars.

I thought, He looks really peaceful.

I lay down on the grass beside Chingwe and gazed into space and tried to make myself peaceful too, tried to let my mind drift. It drifted to thoughts about Martha. About her long brown hair and how nice-looking she was. And how she got worked up about things just like I did but I still thought she was cool, which really surprised me.

I refused to believe we would never see each other again. I thought, I'll find a way. But every time I tried to imagine us meeting, running towards each other like they do in films, Mr le Duke came bursting up out of the ground like some mighty man-mountain and forced us apart.

'Uff, uff.' Chingwe was coughing again—a tiny dry cough.

It broke into my thoughts. 'You all right?' I asked him, sitting up. And that's when I saw it, the vehicle right on the top of the opposite hill.

It had no lights on. But you could see it clearly in the moonlight. It was an open-topped jeep.

I thought, What's that doing there? It was almost as if it was spying on us. Dr Dekler had an open-topped jeep—

Instantly, my mind screamed out: Danger! It was like every nerve in my body was on red alert.

'Don't move, Chingwe,' I warned him.

Chingwe coughed again. In the quiet night the cough sounded like an explosion.

'Shhhhh,' I said, putting my finger to my lips.

He started to whimper. He was scared—he could feel how tensed-up I was.

'It's all right,' I tried to soothe him. 'It's all right.'

Three figures climbed out of the jeep. Their clothes were dark—dark trousers, dark jackets. You couldn't see their faces. They were too far away. Besides, they had some kind of caps on, pulled low down on their heads.

Two of them stayed leaning on the bonnet of the jeep. One

of them moved away from the others and raised something to his face.

I could guess what that was. 'They've got night vision binoculars,' I told Chingwe. They could see us anyway because of the moonlight. But with those they could probably count the zits on my face.

I knew exactly what was going on. I'd even half-expected it.

'It's that creep Dr Dekler—with two of his mates. I knew we hadn't got rid of him. He's spying on us. He wants to kidnap you, take you back to that rehabilitation place.'

I watched the men on the hill. They watched us—they didn't even try to hide.

'Time to make a move,' I told Chingwe.

I shot to my feet, grabbed his hand and started pulling him towards the house. He hooted in protest, 'Ooo-ooo-ooo.' He hated being dragged about.

But I had to do it. 'Come on,' I said frantically. 'We've got to hide you. Before they come down from the hills.'

I hauled him along with me into the kitchen. He was shrieking now, showing his teeth, slapping at me with his free hand. I locked the back door behind us, let go of Chingwe and burst into the living room. Only Pa was there, still busy painting. Ma must have gone up to bed.

'Pa! Dr Dekler's outside!'

'Dr Dekler? What's he want?' said Pa vaguely.

'He wants Chingwe, doesn't he? He wants my humanzee. Look out of the window,' I said pointing wildly. 'You can see his jeep. I know it's him. I thought we'd have trouble with him. I didn't think he'd give up Chingwe so easy!'

Pa finally put down his paintbrush. 'You sure about this?' he asked me.

''Course I am! Do you think I'm making it up? Look for yourself.'

I was already over at the window, yanking the curtains apart.

'He's out there,' I told Pa. 'There's three of them, watching every move we make.'

'How does he know where we live?' said Pa.

'You remember, that form Ma filled in when we left Chingwe—she had to write our address on it, didn't she?'

Pa peered out of the window. 'Where did you say his jeep was, exactly?'

'On top of the hill, just opposite. Three men got out. And one was spying on us with binoculars. It was Dr Dekler, I swear.'

'I can't see a jeep,' said Pa. 'There's nothing there.'

''Course you can. It's clear as anything. That creep Dr Dekler. I'll kill him! I'll—'

'There's nothing there, Nemo,' Pa repeated slowly and firmly, as if he was talking to someone with Spam for brains.

I shoved him aside to peer out of the window myself. Pa was dead right. There was nothing parked on the hill top. No vehicles or people anywhere. In the moonlight the landscape was ghostly and still and empty.

'Look,' said Pa, rubbing his eyes with his hand, 'let's just calm down, shall we? It's been a really rough day. A real pig of a day. First no water and then Chingwe getting sick. Too many problems—Let's get some sleep. Right? We all need some sleep. We're even starting to imagine problems that don't exist.'

'I did see him! I did! I wasn't imagining it!' I was ready to hit something, clenching my fists with frustration.

'Get some sleep, son,' was Pa's weary answer, as he trudged up the stairs. 'Make sure Chingwe settles down OK,' was the last thing I heard him say before he closed his bedroom door.

Fifteen

Chingwe slept at the end of my bed that night. He smelt a bit, sort of sour and musty like an old face flannel. But I didn't mind about that. I wasn't going to leave him on his own downstairs.

I barricaded my bedroom door with furniture. Even looked under my bed, like a little kid checking for bogeymen. I was sure Dr Dekler had been watching the house. That he was trying to snatch Chingwe and that he wouldn't give up without a fight.

'Don't worry.' I patted Chingwe's mangy head. 'I won't let him get you, I promise.'

Chingwe didn't seem worried about Dr Dekler. He opened his mouth like a pink cave and yawned. He scratched himself under the armpits, shifted his stiff old bones about a bit, then fell fast asleep.

I watched him as he grunted softly and moaned in his sleep. He looked so pathetic, so scrawny and scruffy, like a moth-eaten old door mat. The idea of them doing all sorts of tests on Chingwe almost drove me mad. I felt rage and despair boiling up in me just thinking about it. Every evolutionary scientist in the world would want to prod and poke him. He'd be put on display as a great discovery, as the living missing link, when all he wanted was a bit of peace and quiet in his old age.

It'd be nearly as bad as being in that freak show, I thought, bitterly.

Chingwe shuddered in his sleep. His eyelids twitched, as if he were dreaming.

Wonder what humanzees dream about? I thought.

Maybe he was dreaming about swinging through some sunny, leafy, forest canopy back in Africa. Like Pa said, he wouldn't have lasted long. The other apes there would have ganged up against him. Driven him away, even killed him. Still, Chingwe probably didn't realize that—so he still had his happy dreams. Everyone's got to have happy dreams.

I told myself, 'Don't fall asleep.' I had to stay awake. I had to be ready and waiting, to protect Chingwe when Dr Dekler came.

I didn't get undressed. I just lay down on top of the bed. Something jabbed into my hip bone. It was Martha's trilobite, I'd forgotten about it. I took it out of my jeans' pocket and put it on the bedside table.

I thought, What did I do with her drawing of the dino-bird?

Then I remembered, with a little stab of guilt, that I'd gone and left it downstairs on the kitchen floor—and she'd given it to me to look after.

I almost crept down to get it. But I didn't want to leave Chingwe on his own.

Martha would be in bed, in the le Duke compound. I somehow knew that, like me, she wouldn't be able to sleep. I thought, Wonder what she's thinking about right NOW. 'Course, I hoped she'd be thinking of me, just a little bit. But it was hard to guess what else might be going through her mind. Being brought up in the Whirligig Theatre Company was weird. But being brought up preparing for Armageddon must be even weirder.

I thought they were the ultimate *normal* family when I first met them. I could still hardly believe I'd been so wrong.

The night seemed to drag on for ever. I kept dozing off. I didn't mean to but I just couldn't help myself. I got up a few times to peer through the window, checking for Dr Dekler. But I couldn't see any men, or a jeep.

I thought, Where have they got to?

Chingwe groaned in his sleep. His eyelids fluttered but he didn't wake up. Probably dreaming of tree-tops again.

It was getting light, a sort of grey, watery light. And birds were starting to make a racket outside. The long night was over at last.

There was a stale taste in my mouth. My head was fuzzy, my bones were aching. I felt wrecked, like I'd spent the night in a skip.

I took a swig of tonic water from a bottle by my bed. It was supposed to be fizzy. But it was warm and flat. I needed something else to wake me up. I flicked on my bedside radio, surfed through some stations to find some decent music.

'Sad death of Dr Dekler, at his world-famous primate re—'

'What?' I twisted the dial back frantically, trying to hit the station I'd just missed.

'—the fire started late yesterday afternoon in a storeroom at the Primate Rehabilitation Centre. Fire Services were called. But by then, due to extremely dry weather conditions, the fire had spread through the centre and outside to the animal enclosure. More than fifty acres of grass and trees were ablaze. Firefighters found Dr Dekler, overcome by smoke, inside an ape enclosure where he had apparently been desperately trying to rescue his charges. Attempts were made to resuscitate him but he was pronounced dead at the scene. Some animals also perished in the fire but before he died Dr Dekler was able to lead most of them to safety. Tributes are already pouring in to Dr Dekler's pioneering work in rehabilitating captive primates and returning them to the wild. Police say they are treating the fire as suspicious.'

I could see my face reflected in a mirror on the opposite wall. By the end of the news report it had turned sickly grey.

116

It was stupid—the first thing I thought about was Boss. I could see him in my head on the rampage—screeching, thumping oil drums, charging like a mad rhino. I wondered if he was dead too. I couldn't imagine it. All that power and energy just switched off. Click. Gone for ever.

Then I began thinking about Dr Dekler. I saw a dead man. When I saw him last night he'd been dead since the afternoon.

That really spooked me; I couldn't stop trembling. I jammed my hands under my armpits to stop them shaking and took some deep, *deep* breaths . . . Then some kind of common sense kicked in and I reminded myself, 'You didn't actually see him, did you?'

'But it must have been him,' I answered myself.

Pitter patter, pitter patter. I leapt up from the bed. What the hell was that? My stomach scrunched up as tight as a fist.

It was gravel, being thrown against my bedroom window.

'Oh no,' I groaned to myself. 'It's Dr Dekler. I knew he wouldn't give up!'

He'd come back. A living dead man come back to get a living missing link.

I think I went a bit crazy then. There were nightmare pictures screaming around in my brain—of Dr Dekler all crispy black with this ghastly white grin. Like a photo I'd seen once of a soldier in a burnt-out tank.

'Nemo!'

A great shuddering shock went right through my body.

'Nemo!'

Then I realized. 'That's Martha's voice.'

I breathed out a long, slow sigh of relief: 'Phew.' Suddenly my legs wouldn't hold me up. I collapsed on the bed, weak and shivery.

'Nemo, you there?'

I tried to shout an answer but my voice came out as a

feeble squeak. 'Get a grip!' I bullied myself. 'This is no time to go bananas!'

Chingwe was awake. His soft brown eyes stared into mine. He reached out a long arm, clutched at my T-shirt with his black hooky fingers. He looked really worried. But that didn't necessarily mean he was. Those wrinkles across his brow made him look worried all the time.

I needed calming down more than he did. But I stroked his rough fur. 'It's OK,' I told him. 'Dr Dekler can't get you now.'

I pushed myself shakily to my feet, stumbled across to the bedroom window and opened it up.

'Nemo! Where were you? I wasn't sure that was your bedroom.' Martha was staring up at me. 'I've got to talk to you. It's important.' Her voice sounded urgent, really upset.

She was rubbing the scar on her forehead so hard I thought, She's going to make it bleed.

'Come round the front. Just wait a minute and I'll let you in.'

I had to unbarricade my bedroom door first. Chingwe crowded behind me, wanting to get out. I almost told him, 'You've got to stay here.' Then I thought, Why should he?

There was nothing to worry about. Dr Dekler was dead. I even felt sorry about that. People listening to the news didn't know. They didn't know what guts it took to go into an enclosure where Boss was King when a fire was raging. But I knew. I knew he'd died a hero. He was another person I'd been wrong about. I seemed to be making a habit of it lately.

As I was heaving the bookcase out of the way, it flashed through my mind, What about those three men? If it wasn't Dr Dekler, who was it? But I was in a hurry to get down to Martha, so I told myself, 'Could have been hikers, bird watchers, anyone.' I threw my bedroom door open, went rushing downstairs.

At the front door I crouched down and peered through the letterbox. Martha's blue eyes met mine, like they had through the gap in the tree roots, the very first time we saw each other.

Where's the key? I thought, looking wildly around. It wasn't in its usual place on the hall table.

'Hang on, I've just got to find the key,' I told her, through the letterbox.

I started frantically searching, moving the junk around on the hall table. Chingwe got restless, walked through to the kitchen. He rocked along on stiff, spidery legs with his shoulders held back like a marching soldier. He did something 100 per cent chimp. He swiped an orange off the floor with his grippy toes, then swapped it from his foot to his mouth.

Then he turned the key in the back door to go out in the yard. Unlocking doors was one of his talents, like turning grapefruit inside-out and pretending to have a bad leg.

I was just about to tell Martha to go round to the back door when I lifted up a phone book and a key fell out. 'Got it!' I unlocked the front door. 'Hiya!' I was really thrilled to see her.

Martha rushed into the house as Chingwe rocked his way out of it. He left the back door open—he never closed doors behind him.

I locked the front door again. 'Shh!' I put my fingers to my lips to warn Martha. 'Ma and Pa are still in bed.'

I led Martha through to the kitchen. As she slumped in a chair I bent down quickly and whipped her sketch book from under the table. I didn't want her to think I hadn't looked after it.

She looked really shattered. 'I ran all the way here,' she said.

I was bursting with questions, 'Did your dad let you out? Did he change his mind? Why couldn't you see me? What was all that about? What did I do? I mean, did he think I was too much of a show-off, or something?'

She frowned and looked puzzled. 'What are you talking about?' she said. 'You're not a show-off. I thought you were a bit shy, actually. But, anyway, Dad didn't change his mind. He doesn't know I'm here.'

I was amazed. She didn't think I was a show-off. She even thought I was *shy*. Me, Nemo, shy! But I didn't have time to think about it because I suddenly realized what she'd said after that.

'What do you mean your dad doesn't know you're here? Did you run away?'

'I came to warn you,' said Martha. She looked around the kitchen. 'Where's Chingwe?'

'Gone to the toilet,' I told her.

I could see by the startled look on her face what she was imagining. She thought Chingwe was up in the bathroom, sitting on the seat, with the toilet roll close to hand.

'No, no,' I explained. 'He's out in the back yard. That's where he goes to do it, like a dog does.'

'You should bring him inside,' said Martha, looking worried.

'He'd only make a mess on the floor,' I told her, grinning. I couldn't help feeling really silly and light-hearted and happy. Just because she was with me. And because she didn't think I was a show-off—that was a terrific load off my mind.

'Nemo,' she said, in a grim voice. 'Chingwe's in danger.'

'It's all right,' I said, still grinning my big, sloppy grin. 'He's safe now. Nobody's coming to get him.'

'What do you mean?' she said, looking totally bewildered. 'Look, yesterday, right after you left, Dad e-mailed some people. He told them Chingwe was an abomination. That he wasn't a real link between apes and humans. But that Dr Dekler would try to tell people he was. He'd write lies about Chingwe in all the scientific journals. Soon, the whole world would know about him—'

'Dr Dekler's dead,' I told Martha.

I'd stopped grinning now. New suspicions were springing up in my brain like Jack's beanstalk. I thought about Mr le Duke's blue eyes, blazing with righteousness.

And at the same time I thought, He wants to wipe Chingwe off the face of the earth . . .

Martha was still trying to take in what I'd just told her. 'I don't understand it. When did Dr Dekler die. How did it happen?'

'Late yesterday afternoon,' I said, 'in a suspicious fire. I heard it on the radio just now. Those people your dad e-mailed—they must have moved really fast.'

'They wouldn't do anything like that.'

'Did three people come to your house, very late last night, in a jeep?' I asked her. I was winging it now, my mind swooping from one big idea to another. 'Did they? Because, if they did, I bet that was Dr Dekler's jeep. They went to the Primate Rehabilitation place after your dad e-mailed them. They started the fire that killed Dr Dekler, then stole his jeep and came up here to get Chingwe. They're up here now, aren't they? And that's what you came to warn me about!'

Martha shook her head.

'You don't understand. *Two* men came in a jeep. I've seen them before. They helped Dad with the building work after we moved in. They're good people. They wouldn't start a fire or hurt anybody, that's crazy. Anyway, they're not the ones I came to warn you about.'

'I saw *three* men last night,' I insisted. 'One of them had binoculars—they were watching our house. But I know who the third man was. It was your dad, wasn't it? 'Course it was! Your dad wants to get rid of Chingwe. Just because he's a missing link.'

Martha sighed. 'My dad doesn't believe in missing links,' she admitted.

'You can't go around killing things just 'cos you don't

believe in them! And anyway, it's not his fault is it—it's not Chingwe's fault if he's probably a humanzee?'

'But it wasn't *Dad* you saw with the binoculars,' said Martha. 'What do you think it was Dad for? He likes to be peaceable, if he can. It was Mum—'

'Your mum!' I interrupted her. I had a sudden picture in my head of Mrs le Duke's flowery frock and long wavy hair. 'You're kidding me! It didn't look anything like your mum.'

'She had her combat gear on,' said Martha. 'She's the one who really, really hates Chingwe. She loves children, see. She says he'll be used to put wrong, wicked ideas into the heads of little children. She says, "We've got to protect the children!" She told my dad, "Get my rifle!" Mum's the one you've got to be scared of, not Dad.'

I looked at her in total disbelief. I couldn't say anything— I was just gulping, like a goldfish.

'Her combat gear?' I managed to squeak.

'Please, get Chingwe inside.'

But Chingwe was already shuffling through the back door. He'd found a stick and was whopping the chair legs with it.

I locked the back door. Then I took the key out and put it in my pocket, so he couldn't get it. 'Stay inside,' I told Chingwe, sternly.

'Uff, uff,' he went. 'Uff uff.' I was worried about that cough—it didn't seem to be getting any better. He hooted a greeting at Martha, flapped an arm in her direction, took his scabby grey towel, wrapped it around his face and head and sat in a corner like an Egyptian mummy. Then he whipped off the towel so we could see him. 'Hoo, hoo, hoo.' His shoulders shook. It was Chingwe's idea of a joke. Any other time I would have been pleased that he was perking up a bit, getting a sense of humour. But I had other things on my mind.

'Did you say,' I asked Martha again, 'that your mum dresses up in combat gear?'

'Yes,' nodded Martha, as if it was the most normal thing in the world, as if everyone's mum did it all the time. 'She wears it when she's target shooting, practising for Armageddon. She's a crack shot, Nemo. When she's target shooting she gets every shot in the heart. She can shoot the eye out of a rabbit from across the field. And when she's out hunting, she never, ever gives up.'

'She goes out hunting!' I could hear my voice squeaking higher than ever.

'Only rabbits,' shrugged Martha.

I rubbed my forehead. I could feel a stinking headache coming on. I could imagine Mrs le Duke tending sick little rabbits. Not blasting them to kingdom come.

'Christ!' I said in despair. I was out of my depth again, way out this time. 'This is crazy! This is like a nightmare or something. What kind of people are you?'

Martha bit her lip. It was a long time before she answered. 'I don't know,' she said. 'I just thought we were ordinary.'

'Ordinary? You're kidding me!'

'I mean, I thought everyone lived like us. You know, building bunkers, getting ready for Armageddon. I thought all other kids were like me. I thought it was just normal . . . '

'Yeah, well,' I told her, bitterly, 'you've led a really sheltered life, haven't you? If you think that's just *normal*! You didn't even know about dinosaurs. All *normal* kids know about dinosaurs. And did you know your dad was stealing our water. Did you? Did you?'

'No—'

'You don't know nothing, do you!'

'No.' Martha hung her head, as if she was ashamed. And I was ashamed too, for losing my temper and mocking her. It was only because I was scared. I should have known better. I'd been like her too. I'd thought I was just normal, like other kids. Until those three girls had mocked me. Made me feel like some kind of alien freak.

123

'Look, I'm sorry,' I apologized. 'I'm a bit stressed-out at the moment.' I dropped my head into my hands. I felt hopeless. 'What are we going to do?' I asked her. 'Your mum sounds like Terminator or something. She's got weapons. She never gives up! Won't your dad try to stop her?'

'No,' Martha shook her head. 'He couldn't even if he wanted to. She says God wants Chingwe destroyed.'

'That's stupid. I don't believe it! You don't believe it, do you?'

Martha dragged her hand down over her face, as if her mind was in turmoil. I thought, She's still got that stripy pencil behind her ear. Don't know why I noticed the pencil at that particular moment.

Martha finally answered my question: 'No, I don't believe it either. But it doesn't matter what we believe. My mum's on a mission. She's in her combat gear. She's got her rifle. She's got people backing her up—'

'How many people?' I asked her. I was just beginning, dimly, to understand the power of the forces we were up against. It wasn't just Martha's mum and dad. There must be others like them, believing what they did, holed up around the country, around the world, preparing for Armageddon. They helped each other out. They were techno-heads. They contacted each other through the Web and e-mail. They had military style resources. And they moved with frightening speed. I couldn't believe that when I first went into their house and saw Mrs le Duke telling stories, I was really touched—it nearly brought a tear to my eye. It seemed such a cosy scene, so folksy and homely . . .

'Don't take offence or anything,' I said to Martha, 'but is your mum crazy? I mean, if she isn't actually crazy, she must be really mixed up.'

'No, she isn't,' insisted Martha. 'She isn't mixed up at all. She's clear inside her head. She knows exactly what she's got to do—'

'Well, at least Chingwe's safe in here with us. Aren't you?' I turned round to reassure him. He wasn't there. And at the same time as I noticed he'd disappeared, I heard the keys turning in the front door.

'Chingwe!' I yelled. 'Come back here!'

Like I said before, Chingwe was a geriatric hooligan. He was discovering new tricks all the time. I could hear that snorting laugh of his. Sneaking off from right under our noses, then unlocking a door, was his cleverest trick yet.

I ran after him. I couldn't see him outside. The back yard was his favourite place to hang out.

'Go back, wake Ma and Pa up,' I told Martha who was right behind me. Ma had ear-plugs in because Pa snored and Pa was a really heavy sleeper—so together they could sleep though an earthquake. 'You'll have to shake 'em really hard,' I warned her.

I was halfway round to the back yard when I heard the crack of a rifle.

Chingwe was out by the dried-up spring. He had his grey towel dangling from his mouth and with one foot he was whacking the ground with his stick. He looked up when I called his name.

Kerrak!

Right next to Chingwe, limestone exploded like a grenade.

'Eek, eek, eek!' He started this terrible high-pitched screaming. He began staggering about, dragging his useless left leg.

I thought, He's been shot! He's been shot!

I didn't stop to think. Or check where the shots were coming from. I just dodged across that yard. I rugby-tackled Chingwe. Together we crashed into the empty pit, slid right to the bottom, sending up sprays of dust and stones.

Kerrak! I shielded Chingwe with my own body.

The dust died down. Ages seemed to pass. There were no

more gunshots, no sound at all. It was like the world outside the pit didn't exist.

I rolled away from Chingwe. He didn't move; he was curled up in a ball, coughing a rattly cough that made his whole body heave. His arms were folded round his head like a little kid protecting himself from being hit. One hand still clutched that old grey towel. He was stroking his face with it, like babies do.

I shook him frantically. 'Chingwe! Where'd you get shot?'

He opened his eyes. He still had his gibbering fear-face on but I couldn't see any blood.

'Where'd you get shot?' I pleaded, out of my mind with worry.

Chingwe sat up. He plucked at my hair with his stubby fingers as if he was trying to comfort me.

Then I understood. I almost let out a great whoop of delight but stopped myself just in time. 'You faked it, didn't you? Hey, Chingwe, you're a brilliant actor! You did your leg trick, didn't you? You made them think you got shot!'

Chingwe saw a tree root dangling and stretched his long skinny arm up to grab it.

'No! Keep down!' I told him, pulling his arm back.

He chattered at me, furiously.

'Look,' I tried to make him understand. 'There's someone trying to shoot us out there!'

I listened again. I couldn't see the hills from here. Not unless I poked my head out and I wasn't going to risk that. But it seemed very peaceful out there. All I could hear was a skylark trilling away high above us.

'Maybe they've gone away,' I told Chingwe.

Martha slid feet-first down into the pit to join us. 'Keep down! Keep down!' I told her. 'What you doing here! You should have stayed in the house!'

'I'm all right,' she said. 'Are you OK?'

'Yeah.' I was dizzy with relief. 'I thought Chingwe got

hit,' I explained to her. 'I was nearly going bananas. But he tricked them. He's much smarter than they are. Bet they've gone away now. Bet they think their job's done.'

The skylark kept on singing. Martha didn't say anything. She looked tense and pale as death. 'They have gone away, haven't they?' I asked her.

'I don't think so,' she said. 'You don't know Mum. She's still out there. She's waiting. She probably knows she didn't hit him. You can't fool her that easy. She'll be waiting.'

I felt a sudden chill, like someone had walked on my grave. I started shivering. I couldn't help it.

'Where is she, then?'

'Oh, you won't see her. But I bet she's up there. Waiting for a clear shot. I've seen her do it with rabbits. She just sits and waits. She can wait all day. She's really patient. They think she's given up. They come out of their burrows and bang!'

'Did you wake Ma and Pa up? Did you tell them what's going on?'

Martha hung her head. 'I was going to wake them up. Then I didn't. I thought they'd phone the police. I don't want my mum to get arrested.'

'We're getting shot at!'

'She's not shooting at *people*,' said Martha, desperately.

'Yes, she is. She's shooting at Chingwe!'

Martha just hung her head.

'Well, that's great that is!' I said, trying to keep my voice from sounding hysterical. 'We're getting shot at and no one knows about it! No one's coming to help us. We're on our own! So what's the plan, then? I hope you got some kind of plan 'cos I haven't!'

Martha frowned. 'I don't know. We can't take Chingwe out of this pit. Because Mum is still out there. I know she is.'

I didn't think my mind was working but it was because I had a brilliant thought. 'We could take him underground,' I said nodding towards the opening to the caves. 'I don't think he's going to like it—oh, no, I haven't got my torch.'

'I'll get it,' said Martha, scrambling up the side of the pit.

'No.' I tried to pull her down. 'She might shoot you.'

Martha sounded really shocked. ''Course she won't. She's my mum, isn't she? And anyway, she doesn't want to hurt us kids. She believes she's *protecting* us, from dangerous wrong ideas—'

'For heaven's sake!' I spat out, bitterly. But there wasn't time to go through everything I thought about Mrs le Duke and what she believed. So I just said, 'OK, but be careful. Here's the back door key.' I took it out of my pocket. 'There's a torch in the kitchen. On the shelf above the sink.'

She crawled out of the pit and disappeared. I listened, my heart in my mouth, for a rifle crack. I couldn't believe Mrs le Duke would shoot her own daughter. No, 'course she wouldn't. But all the same, there was a tiny, squirming doubt in my mind . . .

Chingwe was huddled up beside me, yipping like he was a little baby monkey: 'Yip, yip, yip.'

Never mind wanting to kill him—it was bad enough that that crazy woman had upset him like this. I hated seeing him upset.

'It's all right. It's all right,' I tried to soothe him. 'There's no need to be frightened.' But he didn't stop yipping. I think he knew I was lying. He seemed really human now, terrified just like I was, wanting to be comforted.

Martha came sliding back into the pit in a shower of pebbles. She had the torch in her hand.

'We've got to move *now*,' she said urgently. 'I saw a black van, up in the hills and some kind of off-road truck with these monster tyres. It's more back-up for Mum, I know it is.'

Sixteen

Chingwe hated it underground—I knew he would. He was frightened of the dark and the cramped spaces.

I played the torch over the stalagmites.

'Look, nothing to be scared of,' I told him. 'Just some old rocks.'

But Chingwe still hooted his distress call, 'Oo, oo, oo.' He gripped his grey towel like it was a life-saver.

'Shhhh!' I told him. I pointed above-ground. '*They* might hear you.'

Chingwe sat and rocked and coughed, hugging himself with his long, spidery arms. I didn't like the look of him. 'Chingwe's sick again,' I told Martha.

She was climbing down the shaft that led up to the empty pit. She'd made two trips back up there, trying to block the hole we'd come through with sticks and rocks.

It wouldn't hold them off for long. Soon Mrs le Duke and the other hunters would get fed up with waiting. They'd come down from the hills to check the pit. They'd see it was empty. And soon figure out where we'd gone.

'They won't hurt Ma and Pa, will they?' I asked Martha anxiously, as she dropped down beside me.

'No, they wouldn't do that.'

'They'd better not,' I growled. I wasn't much reassured. I groaned at the picture that was in my head—of a bunch of people with AK-47s bursting into Broom Cottage. And Ma squaring up to them. 'How dare you bring those guns into my home! Clear off! Or you'll be dogmeat!'

'It's Chingwe they want,' said Martha. She didn't have to remind me.

'So why did they set fire to Dr Dekler's place?' I murmured, thinking out loud. Then I answered my own question. 'I know,' I whispered. 'I bet they thought Dr Dekler had some evidence there, you know, something scientific, to prove Chingwe was the missing link. I bet they wanted to destroy it. They probably wanted him dead as well, because he was going to make Chingwe famous—'

Martha started to say, 'Even if they did start that fire, they wouldn't want to hurt anyone. I think what happened to Dr Dekler was a terrible accident. They didn't want to kill—'

'Oh yeah? So why are they trying to kill Chingwe?' I hissed at her.

I had to bite my lip, stop my mouth from flapping. I didn't want to get mad at Martha. I knew she was on our side.

I realized I hadn't thanked her yet. 'Thanks,' I said, 'for coming to warn us. Me and Chingwe, we really appreciate it.'

'That's OK,' said Martha, half-smiling, half-frowning.

Chingwe whimpered. He was shivering. I hoped he wasn't as clever as I gave him credit for. I hoped he didn't *really* understand that Mrs le Duke wanted to hunt him down and kill him. According to Martha, she was doing it to protect children! What kind of twisted logic is that? I couldn't get my head round it. I gave up trying.

'His cold's come back,' I told Martha.

She was gazing up the shaft, her head on one side, listening.

It was like someone had squeezed my heart. 'What can you hear?'

'Nothing yet. But I think we'd better move further in.'

'What, to the dino-bird cave?' I asked her. 'Down the tunnel? Chingwe'll go bananas in that tunnel.'

I didn't mention how *I'd* gone bananas, imagining Hope Spring flooding back when I was crawling through it.

'But all they've got to do is shift those sticks,' said Martha pointing upwards. 'And look in. And they can see us down here.'

'You're right. We better move. Chingwe,' I said, 'there's a missing link like you. Just along in the next cave. You want to see it?'

'Can he understand you?' asked Martha doubtfully.

I looked deep into Chingwe's brown eyes. They weren't bright any more. They were gummed-up and cloudy. One eye-lid was drooping.

'I don't think so,' I said to Martha.

But, after a bit of coaxing, Chingwe dragged himself after me, up the jumbled heap of limestone blocks.

I shone my torch into the tunnel mouth. 'Look, it's not far,' I told him.

I was certain Chingwe wouldn't go in. But he seemed half-drugged. He didn't make a scene; he didn't scream or stamp or throw rocks. He hardly seemed to care where he was. He dropped on to his knuckles, like proper apes do and shuffled through. I coaxed him along and lit up the way. 'Come on, Chingwe, it's not far. It's not far.'

Things hadn't changed. I was still scared stiff of going through that tunnel. Not for myself this time but for Chingwe. I knew there was something seriously wrong with him. He hated water. But even when his hair got wet from the dripping walls he didn't make a fuss.

I had to help him out of the tunnel on to the floor of the dino-bird cave. I found him a dry, sandy bit.

'Have a rest, Chingwe,' I told him.

I shone my torch into the tunnel to help Martha through.

She came crawling out. 'What now?' I asked her.

I swung my torch up into the great space, high as a cathedral. At least there was an escape route. At the top of the grand limestone staircase was the gap I'd wriggled through to give Martha her sketch book. The other exit from the cave led to the le Duke bunker. That worried me a lot.

131

'Think they'll come that way?' I asked Martha, flashing my torch on the tunnel mouth, high up on the cave wall.

There was no rope ladder dangling down—someone had taken it away.

Chingwe was slumped in a heap on the ground. I tried to cheer him up. 'Hey, Chingwe! Meet another evolutionary bombshell!'

I moved across the cave and aimed my torch at the wall. But the dino-bird didn't leap sparkling into the spotlight. There was just an ugly, jagged hole where he'd been. Someone had taken a sledgehammer or something and smashed him to bits.

'Martha, they've bashed our dinosaur to bits. They've wrecked it!'

My voice was croaky with disbelief. I was really disgusted. What a sick thing to do. I couldn't believe that anyone could trash something so perfect, so beautiful.

'That's terrible,' I said to Martha. 'That's vandalism!'

A few glittering splinters of rock lay in a heap at the bottom of the wall. I picked one up. It was the tiny raptor's claw, the special slashing, retractable one from his heel. Sadly, I put it in my pocket.

'Your dad did this, didn't he?'

Martha didn't answer. She knelt down and picked up a handful of sugary crystals, let them run again and again through her fingers. She seemed in shock, like people after an accident.

'It was him, wasn't it?'

Whoever had done it had used incredible strength, crunching into the rock face again and again, then grinding the bone fragments to powder.

They'd made sure no palaeontologist would ever fix this fossil together again.

Martha was still kneeling. 'I don't know,' she said miserably, shaking her head.

'Well I know,' I started to say. 'I know. It was—'

A strange choking sound came out of the darkness.

'Chingwe?'

My brain exploded into panic. I leapt across the cave, stumbled and ended up sprawled by Chingwe's body.

'Chingwe, what's the matter, mate?' I grabbed one of his leathery hands.

Chingwe was struggling to breathe. His chest was heaving up and down. His eyes were closed. A single tear was rolling down his cheek.

'Look at me, Chingwe! Open your eyes. Martha! Martha!'

Martha was already crouched by my side.

Chingwe's skin was pale, like he was a ghost already. But I couldn't believe what was happening, right there, in front of my eyes.

I rummaged frantically in my pocket. 'Here, have a Polo mint,' I begged him. 'They're his favourite,' I explained to Martha. 'Come on, Chingwe,' I said. 'Stop playing tricks, stop messing about.' I was ripping my ear-ring round and round in my ear. I never even noticed the pain, or the blood.

Martha was crying.

'What you crying for!' I turned on her, savagely. 'He's just bluffing that's all. Like he does with his leg. Just pretending there's something wrong with him.'

And when I turned back, Chingwe was lifting a weary arm, like in slow motion. He dropped the grey towel he used as a comfort blanket over his head, so that his face was hidden.

'See!' I said to Martha, laughing with relief. 'I told you! He's just playing tricks. He's playing hide and seek. He'll take that towel off in a minute and laugh like a drain. It's his idea of a joke!'

Chingwe didn't take the towel off. I thought, He's hiding his face for a long time. His body had gone limp.

I lifted the towel up. Chingwe's eyes were closed. His face

133

had gone slack. I shook him, more violently than I meant to. He flopped about as if he had no bones.

'Here, hold the torch!' I said to Martha. I lifted Chingwe up and cradled him like a baby. 'It's me, Nemo! Stop messing about, Chingwe. That's enough joking. You're making me scared!'

Martha was shaking with sobs.

'What you crying for?' I shouted at her.

Chingwe looked so peaceful. The white torch light circled his head. The worry lines on his face were all smoothed away. He looked as if he was sleeping, dreaming of Africa.

'He's dead, Nemo,' said Martha.

I knew it, anyway.

I laid him down, very gently, on the sandy floor. I took the torch from Martha and switched off the light.

Then I rocked in the dark, backwards and forwards, backwards and forwards, just like Chingwe used to do when he was upset.

'They killed him. They killed him, the bastards!'

But even while I was yelling it, while my cries echoed round the cave walls, I knew in my heart that they hadn't killed him. That he was sick and worn out and very old and probably died of pneumonia.

I switched on my torch again. I shone it on Chingwe hoping that, somehow, he wouldn't be dead. That all this was some terrible nightmare. But it wasn't. It was real.

Martha got up, wiped her face.

'I'm going to tell them,' she said. 'I'm going to tell them that he's dead now, so they can stop hunting for him.'

'Yeah, tell them they got what they wanted,' I spat out, anger burning my throat like acid. 'Tell them my humanzee is dead. That should make them really happy.'

'Are you coming with me?' Martha asked me.

'I'm not leaving him down here.'

'Are you going to take him back to Broom Cottage?'

'Course I am! I thought. What a stupid question.

''Course I'm taking him,' I told her. 'That's his home. Ma and Pa, they love him, like I do—'

I couldn't finish what I was saying. I switched off the torch because I'd started to cry, see, and I didn't want anyone to watch me. I tried to choke back the sobs but they just came out, in a sort of explosion of gasps and hiccups.

Martha waited until I was quiet. Then she said, 'Will you shine the torch up the staircase? I'm going to tell them now—before anybody gets hurt.'

I sprang up, like I'd got the devil inside me. 'Wait a minute! I'm going to tell them too. I want to see their faces. And if they look happy, if they even smile, I'm going to kill the whole lot of them!'

I looked back at Chingwe. He was lying so peacefully in the sand.

'I'll be back in a minute,' I promised him. 'Then we'll go home.' I sniffed and smeared the back of my hand across my face. 'Come on, then,' I said to Martha. 'I'm ready.'

I wasn't really ready. I think I was a little bit crazy. There was just a red whirl in my mind, spinning faster than a tornado.

We climbed up the limestone staircase to the top of the cave. I stood on the last block, with tree roots dangling around my head. I could see slices of blue sky through the hole Martha had hacked out with her knife.

'Give me that knife you got,' I said.

She said, 'No.'

'If they even look like smiling—Please,' I begged her desperately, 'just *lend* it to me!'

'No,' she said. She put her hand on the handle of the knife and moved to the edge of the block. I moved closer, I crowded her.

'I'll throw it down there!' she threatened, pulling the

knife blade half out of the sheath. 'Don't be stupid. If I give you this knife you're going to hurt someone with it.'

Too right, I thought. But I could see there was no way I was going to persuade her. I lost interest in the knife. I flashed my torch back down to the cave floor so I could see Chingwe again. But the beam was too weak. He was lost down there in the dark.

'I'm coming straight back,' I yelled down at him, as if he could still hear me. 'I'm not leaving you on your own.'

We squeezed out into the daylight.

'Where are they?' I said looking wildly round, checking the hills for vehicles.

Martha squinted into the sunlight. 'I don't know. They could still be waiting, in the hills around Broom Cottage.'

'There's the black van!' I'd just spotted it, in the distance, bumping along a track, heading for the le Duke compound.

'Let's check your house first,' I said.

It was like any other normal day, dusty and sweaty and hot. The sun was burning the back of my neck. But I felt really weird, as if I was in cold, cold shadow. My body seemed to be working as normal. My heart was pumping the blood round—my legs were running, climbing. But it was like somebody else's body, not mine. My mind wasn't here where I was—it was back down in the cave with Chingwe.

We ran along a dried-up stream bed. Then climbed up its banks. The white rock crumbled away like meringue. My eyes noticed that particularly—I don't know why.

'Get down,' said Martha suddenly, grabbing me, forcing me to my knees.

'What's the matter?' I looked round, bewildered. For a second I had no idea where I was; what I was supposed to be doing.

'They're there,' she whispered. 'Just down there, inside the compound. The whole lot of them.'

I took a quick peek. Soon as I saw them, I remembered why I was there.

I hissed at her. 'I want to get to those bastards! I want to see their faces!'

They were standing next to the dam, Mrs le Duke and her back-up. It looked like they'd re-grouped. Like they were having a war council, considering their next move. Mr le Duke was there and five or six other men. Two of the men carried rifles.

'Why are we hiding?' I asked Martha. 'Let's just jump right up. Let's tell them.'

'Shhh,' Martha said. 'They've got guns. You don't startle people with guns. Just wait. Just listen first. Come on, we can get closer.'

This was where Martha watched her hawks—she knew these limestone hills like the back of her hand, every crevice and crack. She went wriggling down a gully that took us right to the back of the le Duke compound.

We still weren't close enough to hear what they were saying. But then they started to raise their voices.

'It's the perfect way!' said Mrs le Duke. She sounded on fire with her mission to save the world from Chingwe. Her voice rang out, loud and clear. 'God has shown us the perfect way! The humanzee is hiding down in the caves, we know that. Once my daughter and the boy come up, we'll send the water in—'

'The thing will drown!' interrupted a man eagerly. 'Just as the unrighteous drowned in the Great Flood.'

'And the caves will be flooded,' said Mrs le Duke, sounding thrilled. 'Its body will never be recovered.'

'No!' said Mr le Duke. 'What about the bunker? What about my stores?'

'Your stores are watertight, aren't they?' another man said. 'They won't be spoiled.'

'Give me time to move them!' begged Mr le Duke.

'The stores don't matter!' Mrs le Duke told him. 'God has chosen us to do His work. Do you think He won't provide for us when Armageddon comes?'

'So either help us,' the first man said in a menacing voice. 'Or get out of our way.'

Down in the gully, I couldn't believe what I was hearing. 'They're going to undam Hope Spring!' I told Martha. I forgot to keep my voice quiet. 'They're going to flood the caves. Chingwe's down there—he's all on his own, he hates water. He always hated water. I'm going to get him out of there.'

I leapt up. Martha tried to pull me down. But it was too late. We'd been spotted.

'STAY THERE!' ordered Mr le Duke, in a voice like thunder.

'It's the children!' cried Mrs le Duke. 'They're safe. Let the water loose!'

Men swarmed along the dam. They didn't even wait for the JCB. They tore at the rocks with their bare hands. Then one of them ran to open the steel door that led down to the bunker. Another ran for the JCB. Mr le Duke came striding towards us like an angry giant.

I began to run, like a maniac, back to Chingwe in the cave.

'Come back!' shouted Martha.

'You tell them!' I yelled back at her. 'Tell them he's already dead!'

I could hear her yelling something behind me. Maybe she was shouting to them, maybe to me. But her voice was drowned out by the rumble of the JCB as it went jerking like a yellow praying mantis towards the dam.

I climbed higher. I only looked back once. The men were putting a chain round the tree, to drag it out of the dam wall with the JCB. Soon as that went, the whole dam would explode outwards in a boiling sea of water and mud and rocks. Hope Spring would go roaring down the dry river bed. Then blast through the le Duke bunker—

'Got to hurry,' I panted to myself. 'Got to hurry.'

I slid back into the cave, switched my torch on, half-slid, half-fell down the giant limestone blocks. Then I was kneeling beside Chingwe, on the cave floor.

'Come on, Chingwe, we've got to get out of here!'

I knew that Chingwe was stone cold dead. Only, I just couldn't seem to stop talking to him as if he were still alive.

I didn't know how to get hold of Chingwe. Even though he was a light-weight chimp, he was too heavy for me to carry.

I tried dragging him by the legs. But I couldn't do it. It was too undignified. And Chingwe had been robbed of dignity too often in his life. I thought of him, squatting in that stinking freak-show cage.

Hot tears made my vision go blurry. I screwed my fists viciously into my eyes.

'Stop it!' I raved at myself. 'Chingwe needs you. Don't you dare go bananas now!'

I shone my torch upwards. There was no way I could get Chingwe up that limestone staircase. I'd have to take him home the way we'd come. Back down the tunnel. Up through the dry pit in our back yard. Though I didn't know how I was going to manage the shaft.

I suddenly thought of Ma, staring into the pit, wishing for water. And seeing me with Chingwe's body coming up instead.

I thought, Poor Ma. It'll break her heart. As if mine wasn't broken already.

I put my torch on a rock. The light was only a feeble glow but it didn't matter. Darkness was best for the way I was feeling. I picked Chingwe up under the arms. His head lolled on to his chest like a sleeping baby.

I thought, Whoops. I'd nearly forgotten his grey towel. I picked it up and stuffed it into my jeans' pocket.

I started to stagger backwards. I listened. I couldn't hear

any rushing water. Just the usual drip, drip, drip down the walls.

But, it's funny, I didn't feel as if it was urgent or anything. I wasn't panicking. I was really cool and calm, doing everything in a dream, in slow motion, as if there was no reason to hurry.

It was like another world, down in that cathedral cave. A world that contained just me and Chingwe. Nothing else mattered. Nothing else seemed to exist. I just concentrated on Chingwe, on treating him with respect, on getting him home. I tried to get his body into the tunnel, the one that led from this cave to the cave under our back yard. But I couldn't hoist him up. So I thought a bit, as if I had all the time in the world, then tried another way. I left Chingwe for a second while I went up into the tunnel and dangled myself down and took Chingwe under the arms and tried to lift him up to join me. But Chingwe was a dead weight—he wasn't co-operating.

My muscles were cracking! I was going to have to let him go. I was half-aware of a strange, deep *thrumming* noise somewhere in the caves and tunnels. But getting Chingwe home was all I cared about. So I didn't pay much attention.

I couldn't hold Chingwe—I had to let him go, let him slip back to the sandy cave floor.

'Now what are we going to do?' I asked him.

I shone my torch down from the tunnel mouth, on to Chingwe's body slumped below me. 'Come on, give me a hand.'

A growling sound disturbed the little chat I was having with Chingwe. I looked up, annoyed, shone my torch about.

The whole cave system seemed to be rocking around us. Limestone layers were moving, grinding together. And then, there was a rumbling sound, like faraway thunder.

I had to take notice then. And my mind seemed to snap

140

into focus. I was suddenly back in the real world. The thunder was getting closer—

'It's Hope Spring!'

It was in the le Duke's Armageddon bunker. I could hear it. It wasn't distant any more, it was roaring now, like a T-Rex on the rampage, wrecking the place, splitting rocks apart.

And I hardly had time to react before Hope Spring came through. It blasted like a power hose from the opposite wall, arched in a graceful jet right across the cave. Then dropped to a foaming waterfall that raced in waves like the sea across the cave floor.

It was only then I really woke up, understood the danger I was in.

But I still wasn't going to leave Chingwe.

I balanced the torch in the tunnel mouth, leaned down towards him, reached out my arms. 'Chingwe!'

But the water was already swirling and bubbling all around him. It lifted him up. He was floating . . .

Someone was yelling at me, above the roar of the water. 'Nemo, get out! Get out!'

I knew it was Martha, shouting from the top of the limestone staircase. I shone my torch up there for a split second. And in the time it took to do that Hope Spring snatched Chingwe away from me and carried him off into the darkness.

'No!'

Frantic, I played the torch over the dark, foaming water, trying to find Chingwe's body. I saw a flash of silvery hair, a hand with Chingwe's hooky fingers. Then nothing.

I howled then, threw my head back like a wolf, 'Nooooooo!'

I would've dived down into the flood after Chingwe. I was going to. I leaned right over, it was hypnotic, that dark swirling sea. Slowly, slowly I was tipping myself into it

141

when somebody screamed at me, 'Nemo! Don't you dare! You hear me. Don't you bloody dare!'

I grabbed with both hands at the tunnel mouth, just in time to stop myself falling. For a few seconds I couldn't do anything, except crouch there, trembling. Then I shone my torch upwards. Martha was coming down the limestone staircase with the water rising towards her. There was no way we could reach each other—there was a raging torrent between us. It was slapping off the cave walls, throwing misty spray everywhere, trying to find a way out. Soon, it would find this tunnel.

'Go back up!' I yelled to Martha. She must have hacked away more tree roots—I could see light, even from down here.

She came another step down.

She cupped her hands round her mouth, shouted through the spray and the booming noise, 'Go back down the tunnel. Go back! I'll meet you at Broom Cottage.'

I yelled at her, 'Chingwe!' I swept my arm wildly over the dark flood waters. 'He's gone!'

'We'll come back! We'll come back for him!'

Only that persuaded me to save my own skin. But, even then, I wasn't much bothered whether I lived or died.

I plunged back into the tunnel, twisted round and started to scoot along it on all fours, like Boss making a charge.

I thought, Nemo, you left the torch.

I bent my head round to look back but I saw a white frill, luminous in the dark, chasing after me. Hope Spring had found the tunnel; it was lapping inside—I went loopy then. I stopped thinking about Chingwe. I thought about the layers of limestone above me. Already it hurt to breathe. If I didn't suffocate I'd drown. Trapped in this tunnel by water, drowned underground, alone in the dark. I was crying with terror. I was gasping for air, having a panic attack. Fighting for every breath. My heart was going to explode through my ribcage. Water was rushing, gurgling behind me—

Then the tunnel ran out. I fell out into the first cave, sprawled on a flat rock, dazed and terrified.

I tried to stand up. But water came bursting out of the tunnel after me, dragged at my shoes, lifted me clean off my feet.

I reached up for a tree root, dragged myself clear of the flood, began climbing up the shaft. I wasn't thinking, my mind was in total chaos, I was just moving instinctively up towards the light.

Somehow I found handholds and footholds. I hauled myself up—I didn't know I had that much strength. The water was chasing me, sucking at my shoes.

But it was less violent now. Its force was breaking up. This cave was like a wormy cheese, full of holes—the water had loads of cracks and tunnels to escape through.

My head poked out into daylight, fresh air. The sunshine dazzled me. I gulped some oxygen into my lungs then crawled out of the shaft.

That was it—I was finished—I had no more strength. I just collapsed, helpless in the dry, dusty pit with my eyes shut tight against the glare.

I felt water slide under me. My leg twitched, but I couldn't make a single move to save myself. I was as weak as a new-born lamb.

I opened my eyes a crack. Saw clear water bubbling out of the shaft, then closed my eyes again.

Gently, Hope Spring filled the pool. It lifted me up, taking me with it. I didn't struggle, I just let it carry my weight. I spread my arms out dreamily, floated on its glittering surface. I felt safe, cradled like a baby, floating up and up and up . . .

'The water's back! Look, it's incredible! I can't believe it. Hope Spring is back!'

'Nemo! What are you doing in there?'

'Nemo, you're safe!'

People were calling my name. Their voices seemed to come from very far away. I heard what they said but I didn't open my eyes. I just let myself float away . . .

'Nemo!'

That was Ma.

I sighed. 'You'll have to go back, Nemo,' I told myself. 'You can't float like this for ever.'

So I half-opened my eyes, let sunshine trickle through my eyelashes. Then I opened them properly and saw Martha and my ma and pa all staring down at me.

Seventeen

They helped me out of the water. I stood dripping on the bank and the first thing I said was, 'I'm going back for Chingwe.'

'Where is he?' said Ma.

'Yes, where have you left him?' asked Pa.

But Martha and me were already running.

We couldn't get to him. The cave system was full of water again. All the tunnels were flooded, like they had been for thousands, maybe millions of years.

We tried to get into the dino-bird cave where I'd left Chingwe's body. We tried to reach it from the surface, down the limestone staircase. But the hole that Martha had hacked out through the roots was blocked up with rocks and debris. We weren't even sure where it was any more. We searched for a long time, frantically at first but then more and more hopelessly. Then Martha said, 'We got to give up, Nemo, there's no way into these caves.'

'Course I went bananas and said, 'No way, I'm not giving up. I'm not leaving him down there.'

Martha pushed her hair out of her face, looked me straight in the eyes and said, 'Maybe it's better.'

'What do you mean!' I wasn't in any mood to listen to advice.

'Look,' she said, 'people can't get him down there. He's safe. No one can get their hands on his body, try to find out if he's really a missing link. No humans can mess around with him any more.'

I was opening my mouth to protest, 'I want him back!' But then I thought about the future. A voice in my head said,

145

'Nemo, you can't protect him forever.' What if, years in the future, after we'd buried him outside Broom Cottage, somebody dug him up? Drilled into his bones and his teeth for DNA, put his skeleton on display in a museum for kids to gawp at? Like they gawped at unwrapped Egyptian mummies and Stone Age people dug up from bogs? I couldn't stand that. It would be like the freak show all over again. At least, down in the caves, he'd have some peace, some dignity.

I shut my mouth again, looked gratefully at Martha. 'Think you're probably right,' I told her. 'We should leave him down there.' Even though I'd decided it was for the best, it still hurt me to say it. There was a great raw ache inside me. It got worse and worse while we were searching. Like after the dentist's, when the stuff they freeze you with starts to wear off and the pain hits you.

'Nemo,' sighed Martha. 'I've got to go home now.' She didn't look pleased about the idea. There was a lot of trouble waiting for her there.

I nearly said, 'What, back to the madhouse?' I couldn't help it. I just saw red every time I thought about her mum and dad—how they'd stolen our water; how they'd wanted to hunt Chingwe down and kill him. I'm not a very tactful person; I let my mouth flap. But one look at her face, so grim and pale, made me keep my trap shut. I said, 'Want me to come with you?'

'No,' she said. 'You go home, your ma and pa will be wondering what's going on.'

We smiled weak, worn-out smiles at each other.

'Bye.'

'Bye.'

I watched her trudging slowly off over the hills, as if she had concrete boots on her feet.

I thought, I should've asked her when I can see her again. I was so tired though—my brain wasn't even functioning. It

146

felt like I had a head stuffed with soggy spaghetti. But as I walked back to Broom Cottage I thought, I'd better wake up fast.

I had a lot of explaining to do.

That night—after they'd taken it in about Chingwe and the le Dukes, which took a long time—Ma and Pa and I talked and talked until we were all talked out.

Ma said, 'These people, these le Dukes, do they look as weird as they sound?'

'No,' I told her. 'They look, well, really normal.'

Pa said, 'We should tell the police—if you're sure one of their friends set fire to Dr Dekler's place.'

I looked out of the window of Broom Cottage—the hills were quiet and empty again. There were no jeeps or trucks. Mrs le Duke's back-up had scattered to their own bunkers. And I could hardly believe that, in our own back yard, just that afternoon, me and Chingwe had been dodging bullets.

'I don't know,' I answered Pa. 'I'm not sure what happened any more.'

It was like a terrible dream, being shot at, being trapped underground by rising water, being almost drowned. Except that Chingwe was still dead—I didn't dream that.

We talked a lot about Chingwe. What a pain in the neck he'd been sometimes. And how much we'd miss him. The ache inside me didn't go away. I thought, Maybe it won't go away, ever. But at least my head was a bit more sorted out. I didn't feel crazy any more, like I did just after Chingwe died.

Ma said, 'Remember in the back of the van, when he ate that juggling flea?'

I even managed a laugh. 'Yeah, and remember when he tricked Boss?'

Ma said, 'I'm never going to look at a pink grapefruit again without thinking about Chingwe.'

147

'I wish we'd taken some photos of him,' said Pa. 'We've got nothing to remember him by.'

'Except this,' I told them. And I pulled Chingwe's tatty bit of grey towel out of my back pocket. I put it over my face, whipped it off and did a really good imitation of Chingwe, shaking his shoulders, snorting with laughter.

Ma cried then. She said, 'That grey towel's our most precious possession.'

We knew it wasn't really—our most precious possession was Hope Spring, our own personal water supply. But we all understood what she meant.

Pa said, 'What's to stop these le Dukes damming the water up again, now they've got what they want, now that Chingwe's dead?'

I said, 'I don't think they will. They don't want Chingwe to be found. I heard them talking about it. They want the caves to stay flooded—forever.'

It was late when Ma and Pa and I finally staggered off to bed.

And very early when pebbles spattered against my bedroom window. But I was already awake—I'd been awake for ages, tossing and turning.

'Nemo, it's me,' called Martha from outside.

I lurched across the bedroom, with my head thrown back in a monster yawn. I felt lousy—my eyes were gritty and gummed up. I prised my eyelids open, then gave my chest a good scratch. I glanced down and adjusted my boxer shorts.

Then I opened the window and poked my head out.

'They've shunned me,' said Martha.

'What? What you talking about?' I wasn't feeling too smart that morning. But what she was saying made no sense at all to me.

She started explaining, in a sort of wild-eyed, breathless way. 'I wanted to have a big row about all sorts of things—

about evolution and Chingwe and not being allowed to see you—there were loads of questions I wanted them to answer, loads of things I wanted to get sorted out . . . '

I didn't mean it to but a yawn came creeping up on me, 'Sorry—I didn't get hardly any sleep last night, we were talking about Chingwe—'

But Martha was rushing on, 'They wouldn't answer any of my questions. They wouldn't listen. They didn't get mad or anything, they were just really calm, smiling as if nothing had happened, as if everything was still exactly the same. They said to each other, "This isn't our little Martha talking. This isn't our daughter. It's someone whose mind has been poisoned by wrong ideas." And I said, "This is me. I am Martha!" So they said, "We don't know you. You're a stranger." And they turned their backs and shunned me!'

'What's that mean?' I asked her. 'I don't understand,' I said, suddenly waking up. 'Did they hurt you? Did they! I'll kill them I'll—!'

Someone shoved a mug of coffee in my hand. It was Ma, coming up behind me. Her white hair looked like a loo brush and her panda eye make-up was all smudged—she'd only just got out of bed. 'It means,' said Ma, 'that they're not talking to her. They've shut her out of their lives. They're acting as if she doesn't exist. Isn't that right, Martha?' she said, leaning out of the window.

'Yes, and my little sisters aren't allowed to talk to me either in case I poison their minds.'

She started to cry, big desperate sobs. I didn't know what to say, how to make things better. I was spitting mad at those le Dukes. 'You don't want to talk to them anyway!' I told her. 'They talk rubbish, all about Armageddon and stuff. They're nuts, you know. Me and Ma and Pa were just saying last night how nuts they are—'

'Shut up, Nemo!' hissed Ma, digging me in the ribs with

her knobbly elbow. 'Don't talk about her parents like that. Can't you see she's really upset?'

'I just want them to talk to me again,' said Martha, sobbing. She sounded really tragic.

''Course they'll talk to you again,' I yelled out of the window. I couldn't imagine my family keeping quiet for five minutes. 'They won't keep it up.'

I was trying to be cheerful but she still looked really depressed. She said, 'You don't know them, Nemo. They'll keep it up for years.'

'Come on!' I couldn't believe that.

'Or until I stop having wrong ideas.'

'Look,' said Ma. 'Why are we shouting at each other out of a window? Come inside, Martha, you look like you could do with a cup of coffee. I certainly could.'

I was grateful to Ma, really grateful. She wasn't a very good early morning person—you kept out of her way until she'd had her first fag and about six mugs of very strong coffee. That morning she hadn't even had her first mug but she didn't bite Martha's head off. She was sweet and kind and gentle with her. Like I said before, my ma's unpredictable, she's full of surprises.

We were sitting round the kitchen table when Pa came in. He hung around listening. I didn't take much notice of him at first. I was too busy sorting out Martha's problems.

I'd just had a brainwave, a really class idea: 'Tell you what, Ma, Martha could join the Whirligig Theatre Company, for the summer anyway. You know, until her mum and dad stop being mad at her.'

'They weren't mad at me,' Martha tried to tell me. 'They went round doing all their normal chores, just behaving normally. Except as if I was invisible. They looked straight through me, as if I was a sheet of glass.'

I wasn't listening that hard—I was too thrilled with my

brainwave. I didn't want anything to spoil it. 'It's a great idea, isn't it, Ma? She could come with us, couldn't she?'

Ma would have agreed, I know she would, except Pa came padding over in his bare feet. His eyes were baggy. His face was grey with stubble. He looked more of a wreck than me.

I was saying to Martha, 'You can join the Whirligig Theatre Company. Chingwe was in it. Wasn't he, Ma?'

But Pa was breathing down my neck by now.

'Nemo,' he said, 'it's not as easy as that. Martha can't just come with us. We'd have to ask her parents first, we'd have to get their permission. And first things first, we have to tell them where she is. They must be worried sick—'

'No, they're not!' I burst out, angrily. 'They don't care. They've shunned her. She said so!'

Pa sighed. 'Nemo,' he said, in his warning voice. 'You can't go making these wild promises. All this needs careful thinking about.'

'OK, OK, OK,' I said, trying to calm myself down. 'We'll think about it and *then* she can come with us.'

'I wouldn't object to it,' said Ma, pouring herself another coffee.

'See, Ma agrees!' I turned eagerly to Martha. 'You ought to see me doing Spike's death scene. I'm really good at it, aren't I, Ma? You'll cry your eyes out.'

Ma and Pa got dressed and they went round to see the le Dukes. Pa said, 'I'm sure we can fix all this. There's just been some kind of misunderstanding. I'm sure we can change their minds.'

Pa didn't have a clue what he was letting himself in for. Even Ma didn't.

When they'd gone, I told Martha, 'Bet your mum and dad won't even talk to them. They think we're unrighteous.'

'They think I'm unrighteous now,' said Martha.

She was rubbing at her moon scar like it was aching. I was

twisting my ear-ring round. I didn't know what to say. I was scared of saying something clumsy and hurtful, especially about her parents. I was only just beginning to realize how shocked she was. Sometimes it got stormy with my ma and pa—they gave me a lot of stick. Sometimes we had great big rows. But they'd never done that—behaved as if I didn't exist; as if I was a non-person.

Then Martha said, right out of the blue, 'Do you think Chingwe really was a missing link?'

I said, 'I don't know.' I was telling the truth. Sometimes, when I looked into Chingwe's eyes, I thought he probably was and other times, I thought he probably wasn't.

'Because he might have been some kind of mutant chimp—a cross between an ordinary chimp and a pygmy chimp or something.'

'I know, Dr Dekler said that.' Even though my brain felt like porridge, I made a serious effort then to tell her what I felt about Chingwe. Because, and that's one of the things I really liked about Martha, I thought she would understand—not make my feelings into a big joke. 'It doesn't actually matter to me,' I told her, 'if he was a missing link or not. I mean, I couldn't care less about that. Because, whether he was, or whether he wasn't, he still seemed like a person to me.'

She nodded slowly. 'I got his towel thing here,' I told her. 'You know, the one he carried round with him everywhere.' At that moment I felt that Chingwe was the safest thing to talk about; the thing that drew us closest together. But when I pulled Chingwe's grey towel out my pocket and unfolded it the slashing retractable claw of the feathered dinosaur fell out on to the table. It glittered like diamonds. I'd forgotten all about it.

I'm impulsive, like Ma. So, without even thinking, I picked the crystal claw up and presented it to Martha, 'Have a present,' I told her. I was only trying to make her feel

152

better. But then I thought, squirming, Oh great, Nemo, what have you done now? You don't give girls presents like that! You don't give them dino-bird claws. She'll think you're weird!

But she didn't. She seemed really pleased with it. She even managed a smile. 'Thanks.' She put it in the pocket of her shirt and buttoned the pocket up.

And we sat there, while the morning sun crept further and further into the kitchen. And the funny thing was, I wasn't talking but I wasn't particularly worried about it. Somehow, we didn't need to do any talking.

After a while, Ma came bursting into the kitchen with Pa behind her. Pa was carrying a suitcase. Ma had a red flush on her cheeks. She was hopping mad, I could tell that straight away.

She flung herself into a chair. 'Those people!' she said, as if she couldn't believe it. Her voice was choked up with anger and emotion. 'Those people!' she snarled again, leaping up and prowling around the kitchen.

She would've liked to say more, a lot more—I mean, Ma isn't shy about letting you know what she thinks. But she couldn't this time, not with Martha there.

The nerve in Pa's cheek was twitching—so I knew he was worked up too. But they never told us what happened at that meeting between them and the le Dukes. Pa just said, struggling to keep his voice calm, 'You're coming with us, Martha. We've got your parents' permission, we've got your things here. They said they don't need to see you before you go.'

'Or ever,' said Ma. But she was right next to me when she said it and she muttered it, so Martha didn't hear.

I wanted to tell her, in my showman's voice, 'WELCOME TO THE WHIRLIGIG THEATRE COMPANY!' I thought it was brilliant, something to shout about. I could already see us, travelling round all over the place, having a great time,

Kings of the Road! But Martha didn't feel like I did. She looked so confused and grief-stricken that I told myself, 'Nemo, shut up.' Maybe she thought her mum and dad would welcome her back and forgive her. Fat chance. I wanted to tell her, 'Forget about them, you're better off without them.' I wanted to remind her that they stole Hope Spring, they tried to kill Chingwe. And what about Dr Dekler and his apes? But even I knew it *definitely* wasn't the right time to make my mouth flap like that.

Then Ma happened to glance out of the window. She said, 'There's a post van coming up.'

I rushed to look at it—it gave me something to do. And I couldn't help being excited. A post van up here is a rare sight—we have to go to the village to collect our mail.

'It must be a special delivery,' I told Pa.

'It is,' he said. 'It's the new performing fleas. Better get that cigar box ready, flea handler.'

Eighteen

Our tent was pitched in a bone-dry, dusty field between a bouncy castle and a hot-dog stand. That smell of fried onions was driving us crazy.

Ma and Pa were in the Whirligig Theatre van changing into their costumes—feathery bonnets and moleskin trousers and false moustaches.

Martha picked the juggling flea off her arm with tweezers and put it into the cigar box. We were inside the tent and the first show was due to start in ten minutes' time. The audience, all five of them, were queuing up outside.

'Did you know Chingwe ate the last juggling flea?' I told Martha.

'Do you know,' Martha said to me, 'that human fleas are practically extinct, like dinosaurs? People don't care about that. They only care about cute things or big things like elephants. We should start our own breeding programme. We could end up with thousands and thousands and release them into the wild. We'd be doing the world a big favour.'

'You sure that's a good idea?' I said, starting to scratch.

Martha had got very interested in the biology of fleas. At first, when she came on the road with us, she wasn't interested in anything. She wasn't a natural-born showman, like me. She didn't want to do any acting. And she missed her family, she missed her little sisters. I said to her, 'Aren't you pleased to get away? We get on great, don't we? It's great being in the Whirligig Theatre Company, isn't it?'

But I could see that it wasn't as simple as that for her. She still couldn't believe how they'd behaved. How they'd just cut her out of their lives. It made her really depressed.

Then she saw me feeding the fleas. She said, 'Can I do that?' And her voice sounded alive again, like it hadn't done for ages. So I gave her some tips and she took over my job as flea handler. She was brilliant at it. She kept the fleas alive longer than I could. They were in tip-top condition; the fittest fleas in the world. The chariot racing fleas ran like racehorses. The bicycling fleas pedalled away like Olympic champions.

She started drawing again too. Her sketch book was full of pictures of fleas. They were her new craze, like birds had been before. I don't suppose fleas work for everyone, as therapy I mean, as a cure for depression. But they sure got Martha smiling again.

She was reading biology books too—loads of them. Pa got them for her from libraries and second-hand shops. She was a bigger dinosaur expert than me now, and that's saying something. She kept hitting me with amazing biological facts. Like, 'Do you know wombats have square droppings?'

'Ouch,' I said.

Ma came bouncing into the tent. She had a new peacock feather bonnet on.

I thought, That's a bit over the top.

Martha said, 'I like your new hat.'

And Ma said. 'That girl's got taste.'

Martha talked a lot to Ma. I wasn't even jealous, not much anyway, when I saw how friendly they were.

Pa came in. He started carefully checking the flea circus ring. He checked the tightrope.

'Show time in five minutes,' he said.

'Do you realize,' I told Martha, 'that you've run away with the circus? I thought kids only did that in books or films. But you've gone and done it for real.'

Martha laughed. She put the last flea in the cigar box. 'This isn't a proper circus,' she said.

'What d'ya mean!' I said, pretending to be offended. 'It's got tightrope walkers. It's got jugglers.'

I got serious then. I said, 'You can stay with us, you know, if your mum and dad are still shunning you when we get back.'

'I think they will be,' she said. 'Unless I stop asking awkward questions.'

'You're not gonna, are you?'

'I can't now,' said Martha. 'So I reckon they'll shun me for ever.'

'Who cares? You can stay with us for ever!' I said, as if it was the easiest decision in the world to make. And, to be honest, it didn't seem like much of a struggle to me. I still hated the le Dukes for wanting Chingwe dead. 'You can't go anyway,' I told Martha. 'What would the fleas do without you? You're even better at flea handling than I was.'

'Thanks,' said Martha.

'And I was good,' I reminded her. 'So that means you're class. Maybe the best flea handler ever.'

I desperately wanted her to stay. I was in love with her. I hadn't made a single move yet (apart from giving her that dino-bird claw as a present). I hadn't even told her. Well, how could I, when she was still so upset about her family and everything? But I thought, I'm going to tell her, one of these days.

I didn't even mind her being a better flea handler than me. Because I'd been promoted to musical director. I'd been learning to play the penny whistle. I was brilliant at it.

I opened the tent flap with a flourish.

'Welcome, ladies and gentlemen, to the Whirligig Flea Circus,' said Ma, her peacock feathers wobbling.

I gave out the magnifying glasses. 'Would you like one, sir? And you, madam?'

Martha stood by with the tweezers and the cigar box.

Pa did his warm-up routine, 'And so, ladies and gentlemen, we are the only flea circus in the world by royal appointment. And this medal is pure gold.'

I started to play my penny whistle.

Very gently, Martha put her first flea into the ring.

'And now,' said Pa, 'let the show begin!'

Epilogue

It's a funny thing, but Chingwe's body never polluted our water supply. I mean, you'd expect it to, wouldn't you? Pa was sure that it would. But when he went out to check Hope Spring it still tasted of flowers. He scratched his head and said, 'Nemo, this water should be undrinkable.' But days passed and the water stayed pure. He couldn't understand it.

But I think I understand.

A few days after Chingwe died, I had a dream about him. I dreamed that, after his body slipped out of my grip, Hope Spring took it and cradled him like a baby. The flood water rose right to the top of the cave, rose and rose, taking Chingwe's body with it. It slipped him on to a ledge, right under the roof. And then the flood water dropped. Hope Spring sank back to its normal level, leaving Chingwe behind on the ledge.

Time passed, ages passed in my dream. Water dripped through the limestone, down the cave wall on to Chingwe. Time passed, the millennium came and went. People forgot about the caves. No one could get into them anyway because they were filled up with water. No one disturbed Chingwe's body.

Slowly, slowly, Chingwe's skeleton was coated with sugar-white crystals. It glittered in the darkness just like the feathered dinosaur.

In time, his bones themselves began turning to crystal. Until Chingwe's whole body, lying at peace on the ledge, was a fabulous, sparkling jewel.

Other books by Susan Gates

Raider

Now in mass-market paperback
ISBN 0 19 271752 9
Commended for the Carnegie Medal

When Flora and Maddy start to research the history of the *Arctic
Raider* as part of their school project on the local fishing industry,
they stumble upon a mystery. Why did a member of the crew die
on his first trip? Who was the mysterious captain, The Iceman?
Just what did happen on that cold Christmas Day aboard the
Raider?

' . . . it is still possible to find new fiction that can be read even next
year, or later, or twice by the same reader. *Raider* is one for a start.'

The Observer

'The characters of the girls are accurately drawn and you will be
desperate to read on to the end.'

The Times

Iron Heads
ISBN 0 19 271755 3

'No! Don't go into the fog! You'll never find your way out!'

When Rachel's parents get jobs on an offshore island, her main worry is when the wind turbine will be installed so that she can play her CDs. But then she notices some weird things happening. Her brother, Stevie, always untidy, insists that everything in his room should be in straight lines, facing the same way. The island rabbits dig their burrows in parallel lines, facing north. Why don't the Islanders get lost in the fog? And why did the last warden's house burn down? As she tries to find the answers to these mysteries, Rachel has to act quickly to prevent another tragedy.

'This book is both exciting and thought-provoking.'

Books for Keeps

'an adventure story, realism and fantasy excitingly blended.'

The School Librarian

Firebug
ISBN 0 19 271735 9

Callum crouched in the blackest shadows of the alley-way. He was gazing intently at the front door of the house across the street. It was crazy to hang around here. But he just couldn't help staying to watch.

When Callum set fire to his own home to take revenge on his mother's boyfriend, Nick, he had no idea of the disastrous chain of events he was to set in motion. Who was the weird android-like figure crouching by the incubator at the chemical company where his dad works? Why was his dad having secret meetings with Nick? And what was happening to the trees in the forest? Throughout all these strange events, the squirrel seems to be the only thing Callum can rely on.

'Surreal events balanced by psychological insight make this redoubtable story of pyromania a truly enlightening thriller.'

The Times

'a super book for 11 to 14 year olds . . . The narrative moves between exciting, vivid descriptions of the action and moving descriptions of Callum's emotions.'

School Librarian

The Scavenger's Tale   Rachel Anderson
ISBN 0 19 271736 7

Some time in the future, London is a post-war zone, suffering disease and decay. Bedford and his sister Dee scavenge from bins in the centre of the city. It's dangerous work. You could be picked up and sent to a Classification Centre and if you're a Dysfunc, you might never come back.

Dragon's Rock   Tim Bowler
ISBN 0 19 271693 X

For Benjamin sleep had become a place of fear, where the dragon with its roaring fury hunted him. But now he had the chance to go back to Dragon's Rock and put things right. And then maybe the dragon would leave him alone.

River Boy   Tim Bowler
ISBN 0 19 271756 1

It didn't start with the river boy. It started as so many things started, with Grandpa, and with swimming. It was only later, when she came to think things over, that she realized that in a strange way the river boy had been part of her all along, like the figment of a dream. And the dream was her life.

The Sea Serpent   Frances Calvert
ISBN 0 19 271739 1

Helena becomes involved with the Serpenton amateur dramatic
company who are putting on a play about a local legend, the sea
serpent. But soon she begins to notice something very odd about
the company.

Dark Thread   Pauline Chandler
ISBN 0 19 271761 8

Kate is a weaver, like her mother. When her mother gets killed,
Kate knows it's her fault. If they hadn't been arguing, if she hadn't
crossed the road when she did . . . Grief and guilt come together in
a visit back in time to the mill, when Kate learns to weave the dark
thread in her life: the sad things, the black parts, which make the
rest of the pattern stand out and make sense overall.

Against the Day   Michael Cronin
ISBN 0 19 271760 X

It is 1940 and the Nazis have just invaded Britain. Two boys, Les
and Frank, find themselves caught up in the Resistance
movement. On Hitler's birthday, when every town and village is
forced to celebrate, the fight-back begins. And the boys find
themselves in the middle of a dangerous game.

Tightrope   Gillian Cross
ISBN 0 19 271750 2

Ashley's life is full of drudgery—until Eddie Beale notices her. Eddie looks after his friends, but only as long as they entertain him. At first, Ashley is happy to put on a show. Then she realizes that there's another audience. Someone is stalking her, and the messages he leaves are getting uglier and uglier. Can Eddie help? And if he does, what price will she have to pay?

The Lost Mine   Pamela Grant
ISBN 0 19 271659 X

Jamie has always known that he cannot go underground into the mines. It is his worst nightmare; the secret fear that has haunted him all his life. But he also knows that when he is fourteen, without fail, the Company will send him deep down into the earth. There is nothing else for Jamie to do in this mining village, and if he doesn't work his family won't eat.

It's My Life   Michael Harrison
ISBN 0 19 271749 9

Martin knew something was wrong as soon as he stepped into the hall. He should have turned and walked straight out again. But he didn't and within minutes he finds himself in the middle of a nightmare. He is kidnapped and held captive on a canal boat—but that is only the beginning. When Martin finds out who his kidnapper is, and who he is in league with, the horror deepens and Martin has to use all his ingenuity to escape—with Hannah's help.

166

Plundering Paradise   Geraldine McCaughrean
ISBN 0 19 271547 X

Nathan felt his blood throb. He and his sister were going to live among pirates and savages—live out the stuff of dreams on a far-away island! But does paradise or hell await Nathan and Maud on Madagascar?

Forever X   Geraldine McCaughrean
ISBN 0 19 271748 0

When their car breaks down, the Shepherd family have to stay in a hotel called Forever X. Here they celebrate Christmas every day of the year. Complications arrive when Mr Angel lands up in a tree, when the police arrive looking for the Starrs, and when Santa Claus escapes in a bus.

Stones in Water   Donna Jo Napoli
ISBN 0 19 271798 7

Roberto and his friends are snatched from a cinema in Venice and taken to work for the German army. This is the story of how they endured starvation, beatings, and freezing temperatures, and of how some of them survived.

Witchy   Ann Phillips
ISBN 0 19 271794 4

Thrown out of home on suspicion of being a witch, twelve-year-old Aggie has to make her own way in the harsh world of the Fens in the 1890s. But wherever she goes, the gossip follows her, until she almost comes to believe it herself. 'If I got seeing and knowing,' she asks her gran, 'am I a witch?'

Aggie hopes she can put the past behind her and make a new life for herself; but then comes news from home and Aggie is thrust back into a life of superstition and hate.

Sweet Clarinet   James Riordan
ISBN 0 19 271795 2

Billy thought growing up in wartime was fun. But then a bomb fell directly on to the shelter where Billy and his mother had gone to take cover. Billy wakes up in hospital, horribly burned and longing for death—until a precious gift from a soldier, who is also disfigured, gives him hope and a reason to go on living.

Starlight City   Sue Welford
ISBN 0 19 271791 X

It is the year 2050. Something is just beginning that will change Kari's life for ever. It will take her to the City, a place where she could be killed for the clothes on her back. What is it that makes Kari and her friend Jake brave the terrors? All she knows is that she has no choice . . . going there is something she must do, even if she doesn't really know why.